NOTHING LEFT TO FEAR FROM HELL

A note on the author

Alan Warner was born in 1964 in Oban. His 1995 debut, *Morvern Callar*, is a contemporary classic. He has won the Somerset Maugham award and the James Tait Black Memorial Prize, was nominated for the Booker Prize and was picked as a Granta Best Young British Novelist. His other novels include *The Sopranos, These Demented Lands, The Deadman's Pedal* and *Kitchenly 434*. He teaches creative writing at the University of Aberdeen.

Also by Alan Warner

NOTHING LEFT TO FEAR FROM HELL

A Surreal Chronicle

Alan Warner

Polygon

First published in hardback in Great Britain in 2023 by Polygon,
an imprint of Birlinn Ltd.

Birlinn Ltd
West Newington House
10 Newington Road
Edinburgh
EH9 1QS

www.polygonbooks.co.uk

1

ISBN 978 1 84697 569 1
eBook ISBN 978 1 78885 530 3

Typeset by 3btype, Edinburgh

For Kenny Lindsay – a great writer and old friend

Chapter 1

Not even a breeze remained as the boat came out of the west in the weird silence, bowsprit broken away and cast overboard, sail lashed, rising and dipping oars sounding like the slap of linen shirts on riverside stones.

Onshore, mist thinned then thickened. Dropping oar blades were extracted, drawn over their thole-pins and stowed as the vessel came shoreward. A blunt phalanx of fumes manoeuvred from the outcrops of the low island, snuffing its colours down to a bulk.

A shore emerged from the briny effluvium, black rocks capped with scalps of wet kelp; sea-wrack crammed the stone gaps where the surface minutely swelled and the water became clear as good glass; behind this shore, higher up, sponges of bleached pink moss and peated moor tundra showed. A soaked island.

Suspended in the air was drizzle that seemed to both rise from the ground and fall from the bland zenith; in not a second, inseparable from the dancing steam clouds, a dust of tiny midges manifested in bouncing puffs. Some large bird above – no gull – was just a swift shadow in the cloud and then gone. Perhaps an owl?

The twelve men aboard the wooden craft were united in one collective, speechless action – they all glared with huge intent at whatever was, or could be hidden, in the landward coils of vapour.

The battered, fibrous bow wood made a dull thud hitting the rocks, and a man came down off the breast-hook very skilfully, one leg bent to absorb his landing; he wore heavy, sodden trews trimmed with buckskin. A horse rider, then. But his knuckles were snow, his feet were bare, pruned by the hard wet night crossing, perished-looking; he seized the dripping bow rope and searched for somewhere to tether, but there was nothing in this worked-over shoreline of stone. He used his full weight on the rope, as if heaving in a tug of war, trying to keep the prow point-on, preventing a yaw sideways, which made for a better musketry target.

Two more men came down, and one momentarily slipped to a knee on the wet stone. But he made no oath: just rose promptly, taking the rope, as did his comrade. With a sword tethered hard across his back, a stout older man, surprisingly lithe, jumped down onto the rock and spun round, held out a hand to offer assistance, but the tall pale man above him descended by placing his palm on the wood and he landed soundly on his feet. 'Your good prayers worked, Father,' the pale man declared. His voice was soft and weary, with an accent that was British but sounded odd. He wore a plain ochre coat, heavied by drenching, with fine blue working on old cuffs, a rough blanket round the shoulders.

The portly, armed figure danced aside and then inland; his flighty movements seemed to suggest both extreme awareness and brute defence. His bonnetless skull of wild grey hair moved to left and right like the flaps of worming sea kelp at the shore. More men came down off the boat and they tethered the rope by carrying in a large boulder to bind it round.

The pale man stepped forward then halted abruptly on a section of staired rock, mapped out with yellow crotal. Tipping his face forward from his slim neck, in a curious, not inelegant stance, he vomited liquid, spat, then sicked up much more, along with a deep eruption of stomach wind; this returning hit the stone all about his gaitered feet in splatters, but he made no effort to shift from his own inundations.

Of the watchers, one extremely youthful character, Calum, youngest of the boatmen, stared curiously and spoke in a low voice, pointing at the rock surface. 'See now, sire.'

The pale man smiled through teary eyes, breathed out a chuckle and raised a hand to slap at the midges already settling upon his face.

'Blooded flux, sire. You must immediately take great care to yourself.'

'Peace on your tongue, child, no flux here,' said the sword carrier, who had returned out of the mist.

The pale man spat again, smiled, spoke once more in his thoughtful, quiet voice. 'You will be an apothecary yet, young Calum, but you mistake returned Burgundy for royal blood.'

'Ah.' The young man let his mouth drop, understanding. 'Forgive me.'

Both the older men now smiled wryly, glancing one at the other.

'I would say to pass the same bottle now, my fine fellows,' the pale man said, 'but it's not all that must be out me. Fouler elements of water need beyond.' He grunted, peeled the blanket from his shoulders and threw it far aside as he suddenly crouched, hoisting his coat and lowering his trousers. With startling force, a rope of brown liquid shot out and continued to spool from between his bared white buttocks. 'And the midges will eat better than us upon my arse.'

Someone laughed.

'Wheesht' was the response from the bonnetless swordman.

'Bring me rags again, fellows.'

Donald MacLeod, the old boatman, who still stood high on the bow, threw some damp fabric down to the swordman, who called in a louder voice, 'Up, take heed, danger is everywhere. Eyes anywhere.' He gestured impatiently with a hand. Two men with pistols went very fast onto the low slope then away from the shore till mist took them. 'Do you know this place, Donald?'

'Aye. Sound coving, four can pull in.'

The kneeling man bent forward with his underthings taut below his pale shanks while the bareheaded man with the sword stepped quickly ahead, holding out the cloth at arm's length. The pale man took it, wiped, then sent the corrupted rag away into the water before he raised his trews.

The man with the sword, and the others too, had already moved away from him. Donald was crossing repeatedly between each gunwale, looking down into the water on both sides as if to judge submerged obstructions.

The pale man walked forward a step or more then sighed. 'And now I must pish,' he told no one, facing into the mist. He fiddled daintily at his loins and sent out a steady stream before him. 'Not that I was ashamed to pish out on the water, my good friends, but it was the standing I failed in.'

The swordman returned out of the mist again. 'It's another settling here, sire. Nothing but away from the shores on this side. Choosing wisely is the way – into the

declensions and seek fresh water for us all. It's sorely
needed with some shelter.'

'Aye. Aye, O'Sullivan,' the pale man said, elongating
the syllables. 'I am more at home on earth already. Is night
close?'

'No, it is morning-time, sire, hours or more. A poor
choosing either way; we must take ourselves up away off
this shore. Boys,' he called out. 'Three of you. Back
aboard and shoal this out where Mr MacLeod tells you,
please. Quick now, before this murk is gone and eyes are
on us from all sides.' He blinked out into the mist. 'It's
more the sea torments me. They seek us from land also,
but sea is the greater evil of this place. We will be undone
if they spy where we land here.'

These desperadoes moved back from the shoreline then
down onto a south-facing shore. Here, in the open and
dragged free of the shingle into the machair, was a rotten
and upturned boat, holed in its keel. They propped it up
enough on the landward side and took turns to sleep
beneath it when the rain came. Puddle water was fetched
from pools in green Burgundy bottles. A night watch of
sentries revolved. They dared not set any fire on an open
coast, so their inundated clothes remained soaken.

The pale man slept in a ragged, damp sail, which he shook free of earwigs and sand jumpers, pulling the stiff fabrics around him, a neckerchief across his face against midges, chuckling and murmuring beneath the garment in other languages, till sleep took him.

Chapter 2

The Prince, O'Sullivan, Father Allan Macdonald and Ned Burke, on an afternoon trek to the latest embarkation, came upon a lone, lowly blackhouse of haphazard clods atop low walls. Moated by a glistening ring of puddled, fresh wet muck, the dwelling appeared as a thing erupted up out of the earth itself, risen from ages of stone before written histories.

Nothing moved but the hearth smoke, which idled at the side of poor damp turf roof and birch thatch – until a hunched beast broke from the rear, sideways, trying to make straight out into the peat bog: dark cloakings, scarf-muffled mummified skull. So stooped and so stunted was it that each man momentarily took it for a black sheep or hog. Yet O'Sullivan lowered his hand, which had shot to his sword hilt, and he was upon that creature in a few hasty steps. 'Hold up, woman. Hold up.' He spoke some words of Irish. It turned its terrible head to him then upon them all. Its face was as midden black as the bog puddles. A terrible frown cracked along the brow, showing some tender pink in a single serration, like the glistening raw streak against the charcoal of barbecued mutton, skewered fresh and smoking from fire.

'This is a mad woman or witch,' the Father forewarned. 'Living in chosen hermitage. Scorned.'

'What pity,' the Prince said. 'Bring her by me.'

'These creatures bite, sire.'

Ned cautioned, 'Or sweep rags away to leave naked sights hard to cast from memory.'

The Prince laughed. 'Look, my fellows, O'Sullivan is feared, he who fears no man. He will kill men, yet this Irishman goes canny with a she-thing. He who stands firm on two feet when a tall dragoon comes at him on a white horse.' He turned a laughing, imploring face to his accomplices. 'I have seen his bravery with my own eyes, but today he meets a match.' He called out, 'Give her a penny, for Christ's sake, sir.'

The Prince crossed deliberately to Ned and intimately addressed him, so the younger man visibly stiffened at this private bestowal. 'Ned, hear this.' The Prince spoke in a virtual whisper, face close up to Ned's cheek. 'An Englisher dragoon near Carlisle was come through too far at our rear. O'Sullivan, caught off his horse directing our men, came around on the safe left side of the devil, cleverly took his sword point and, as if spearing meat from the campaign fire, put his point in where the dragoon's tall boot ended and stocking began. He pushed forth the blade point, and the squeal of a girl came from that English boy's mouth. That big English rider's sword was brought down, and, in midst of such danger, he simply sheathed it in scabbard and dropped rein; his horse circled, and that rider began to feel at his fresh wound with his bare fingertips. A curious sight and, save for prisoners and taken officers, as close as enemy ever came to my person in hot heat, for I had drawn my fine sword too, to find it resting in my hand without reckoning it there.' Cautiously he added, looking around them, 'Though surely this closeness to the enemy could change any day now, if I am to be taken? Aye, Ned. That Englishman sat in saddle at middle of that lively mêlée as if he never knew what war was, until the sharp wound brought him from his sleep, leg out of stirrup, making quadrilles with his foot and his toes to test its remaining possibilities for a future dance in some great ballroom.' He laughed. 'Then the cheeky brave scoundrel trotted to their rear as we mocked cruelties after him, his commander and king.'

The helpless primitive was being led back towards them by O'Sullivan, utilising a mix of gestures and gentle encouragements to her left shoulder with his sword hilt – the long blade harmlessly dropped to the vertical, so that he did not have to touch her with his own gloveless hand. He repeatedly curdled his nose, flicked his head sourly backwards at the wafts of her vibrant spoor. The hems of her sacking shroud were a sodden mash that dragged over heather clumps, so the creature's means of phantom locomotion beneath were invisibled. Her dark mask fell to uneven ground then defiantly rose, and she gave them all mad white eyes.

Her arthritic hands were also reptilian black, but for the lunulas and nail plates which for some reason – pruning shellfish, perhaps – were perfectly clean, so even the pale cuticles showed, high and pink against the ancient grime of her ways, the fingers as innocent and somehow tenderly human as those of a bairn.

'Come, sir, we smell no sweeter, for sure.' The Prince beckoned. 'Stand restful before me, madam. No danger here. I predict you know it not. I am my father's son, your prince and true king-to-be, and you my loyal subject.'

She made sounds like a frighted dog, and the Italian prince before her blinked. 'What does she say to me in your good language, Father?'

'That isn't our language, sire.'

She farted massively like a gun horse, and there was a gurgle from her midriff, muffled by her vast slag of layerings. O'Sullivan stepped further back.

The Prince smiled. 'Do I hear there a loyal prayer to King George?'

These pirate men all laughed, that dangerous, unified mirth of men.

The Prince sighed. He stood straight and surveyed all around him: the ghastly hovel and these flat islands of forever, a vast treeless stage, unhinged of purpose and formed out of absence. 'So much fear in one with so little to lose in this world, bowels loosed when the fear should reside with us fine fellows. We, who have nothing left to fear from Hell, which seeks us everywhere. Strange, no?'

She fell to her knees so completely, the Prince took the flattery. He stooped low himself, spoke softly to her, holding up a hand. 'Hush, madam, you have less to fear in me than from the robin bird at winter.'

O'Sullivan had come by his side, wary and defensive should any small offence be displayed; with his calf pouch he fumbled rapidly, producing the smallest coin he could select, and he then handed the currency to the Prince.

The woman's eyes swiftly had the coin locked in very sane recognition. The black, sooted hand of a chimney clamberer reached out, the palm trembling, and the claw closed instantly on the alms which the Prince cautiously dropped to avoid her touch. Her head nodded in pleased acceptance.

'Is coin of any use in this rough place, my men?'

'Never far to go in this world to reach a place where money comes of use,' the Father stated.

'How do you eat, madam?' the Prince frankly enquired. 'Teach us something.'

Ned's voice, ever located behind his master's back, asked, 'Might she have in there meat or bread?'

'Bread? Hah!' The Father looked at the blackhouse. 'Her walls may as well be hung with coloured jewels from the Orient.'

The Prince straightened suddenly and the woman flinched. 'How could we take even a crust from her, my men?'

The Father nodded obediently but still said, 'Ned, look inside.'

The Prince kneeled again to study his latest object of interest. 'Have you no family here, madam, no daughter or kin? Father, ask her to tell me how she eats in this drearily chosen spot.'

The Father came forward and spoke Gaelic loudly, as if he were shouting warnings into a dark cave. 'Ciamar a tha ur stamag?' The woman was looking up at him in some amazement. Suddenly, she answered in a voice calibrated through the incursion of smoke. Then she fell silent once more and crossed herself repeatedly. Then she spoke again at some length with trembling, petrified pauses. Everyone waited. Still leaning forward, as if he were cautiously peering over the huge cliff edges of Trotternish, the Prince asked quietly, 'What does she speak of, sir?'

The Father coughed. 'The beautiful she-creatures of

the ocean crawl out of the water at night and bring her food.'

Ned was at the partly collapsed arch of the entrance to her dwelling, barricaded by something that resembled an ill-fitting door: crossed boards of faded driftwood fused with warped boat planks, hinged to the jamb by lashed and frayed ropes. Young Ned called back, 'Selkies and mermaids. Well, I hope they come in daylight too.' He tugged and rattled at the ramshackle hatch.

The woman's head swung around, alarmed.

'Take care,' O'Sullivan shouted, without looking away from the huddled woman. 'An armed man could be within.'

The Father spoke again in Gaelic – to reassure her, it would seem.

'Why does she make life here, Father? I see no natural advantages of such a place.'

'Why anywhere, sire? The pickings are the same. Her ancestors and those before will have been rooted in this spot.'

'Tell me more of her curious sea creatures.'

'Lack of food fevers her disabled mind, sire.'

'Oh, come, come,' shouted Ned. Smoke rioted out of the forced doorway to the blackhouse, and the young man waved his arms before his face then cautiously ducked into the woman's quarters.

'It knows how to set a peat fire, sure,' O'Sullivan said, nodding.

'We could make use of fire for an hour.'

'It is all with such hazard, sire,' O'Sullivan replied. 'One of us must keep watch if so, then swiftly onward. Never tarry, never tarry, we need to make for the boat.'

The Prince turned to him. 'What if troopers and an English officer come and learn she harboured us? Would they sack her?'

The crash of an overturned pot came from within the blackhouse.

'I fear they would think the work already done, sire.'

'Would they make sore sport of a crone like this, Captain O'Sullivan? Those men?'

Ned walked backwards out from the fuming doorway, as if conjured onto a magician's stage, followed by a vertical body of signal smoke which peeled from him upward and evaporated. He wiped his eyes, lifted the door closed again.

'What, no plump goose hung and plucked?' the Father asked.

'Troopers will make sport of anything, sire,' O'Sullivan said.

The Prince chortled. 'No, no. It is unthinkable; we cannot fight such an enemy as would consider it.' He stared at the crouched woman, her breathing so distressed.

O'Sullivan said, 'They would tumble her shoulders into an open barrel on its side, sire, so as not to see the grannie face, toss buckets of water on the rump end to freshen and pintelise her regularly, making use of both vents there – it's the way of war for scummish troops.'

'O'Sullivan!' the Prince protested, then laughed. 'We would as well take our waving doozies onto a formed and smoking dung heap, poke a hole and have pleasure with that.'

'That's the English for you, Highness.'

The Prince frowned. '*Attention, ne parle pas comme ça devant le garçon.*' He nodded at Ned, then looked all around, growing restless already.

'Nothing,' Ned reported. 'Though the darkness is so thick you need to live a week there to permit vision. When I say nothing, nothing is meant, save the fire, used seashells, damp peat clods. And a pot.'

Father Allan shrugged. 'Donald has a big pot he brought from Morar in the boat, wise man.'

'Aye, I bailed sea water long enough with the damn thing, and there's been nought to place in it since. Maybe the redcoats have already been here? Ask her.' Ned slapped at the cobwebbed arms of his overcoat.

'Tell me more of the mermaids of the sea,' the Prince suddenly demanded, a straight prurience in his voice, turning on the woman. 'Were they handsome in form, and clothed or unclothed?'

'Sire, little time to talk of spooks with a witch.'

'Spooks, sir? Come. What is she to ourselves but a spook? This world has made her so – an imp who lives the nights here for year on year. Imagine, sir. Imagine, we all of us would move among ghosts tethered to this place for long.'

The other men listened obediently then allotted it a place in their considerations of life and this man.

The Prince kneeled fully with a meditative thumb under his chin. 'Madam, let it be known we did you no harm and, moreover, I promise you this. It is fact that soon I will return with a full French army to join with the still-hardy ranks of my army here, and I shall carry gold enough for all; I will find you and ensure you live with the comfort that should be afforded a Christian in your native place. Remember me this. Mark this place. Tell her, Father, tell her true.' He flicked his hand at her, but he simultaneously rose, turned his back on them all and strode ahead towards the coastline.

The Father coughed and stepped in closer to the crone then declaimed words the Prince would never know.

❦

These men, death's border guards, vain popinjays with their occasional bright colours, prancing around her, now proceeded north towards the shore, and the old woman watched them recede from her domain and precincts. Her tunnelled eye sockets followed in the familiar hold of a cat or a seabird, while she caressed the coin in her gnomish claws, staring out from where she would do most of her knowing of this world until, soon, her quitting of it. An end without conclusion or human witness, where something called nature, or God, tried to reckon the justice of it all.

꧁꧂

Later that night, after their tense crossing to the shoal waters of the next island, Ned had him alone and said, 'Captain O'Sullivan, sir. His Royal Highness told me today of your brave deed on the field with the single dragoon.'

'What deed is this?'

'I am unknown of where it was committed. By the place called Carlisle, did he say? When on foot you poked the fine dragoon's leg with your sword end. He rode off nursing the blow as you all mocked him.'

O'Sullivan frowned, looked over towards the Prince, who was waving his arms, dancing and jesting with the others, and lowered his voice. 'His Highness is mistaken, Ned. That was Fitzwilliam's move. Tops Fitzwilliam, from Gallowmore. Not I. Strange he should attribute it to me.'

'Oh. Excuse me.'

'He has endless wars in his head, boy. Don't trouble him with your need for a fount of tales. We are in a fine

enough tale today for all your children to be told – if you
live to have children and tell it. I have a French commission,
lad – you not – so don't end on a tight rope in London,
if they bother to carry you so far.'

Chapter 3

Clanranald ducked as he entered the ruin. John O'Sullivan was holding aside a rough jute curtain that shiny globules of tossed-up muck clung to, like the shells of black beetles. The Prince, stood already, smiled. Clanranald had a memorable way of moving daintily, as if dancing – as if life was a game. He came across the rough earthen floor of the hut in just such a manner, bowed, swept aside his right arm, a flourish of the bright red bonnet hanging there, and said, 'My Royal Highness . . . My Royal Highness, Most High Royal Highness . . .' He clicked his face into a new mode. 'Bewail. This situation defending Inverness. A hard coming for you, sire. I come with Neil MacEachain, a schoolmaster and my children's tutor. Trusty. A French-speaking boy for you, trained with priests in Douai.'

The Prince nodded, kissed in greeting, clutching
Clanranald's upper arms with his own two hands, and told
the chief – in English – how gladdened he was by his
presence, and then asked cautiously after his son.

Clanranald soon went on: 'I infer you might consider
your presence here a disbenefit. But, sire, everything I can
do. Everything.'

'Yes, yes. Heartening, but sit, sir, sit, and we shall talk.
There is mutton – cold. I am afraid we killed a scrawny
cow and remain unsure who we pay.'

'You need provide me with nothing but your safe
presence, sire. I offer you fresh biscuit from my kitchens.'
He fired out his right arm again, and in it, wrapped in thin
cloth, were forms of biscuit.

'Biscuit?'

'Aye. Biscuit, sire. Good butter biscuit.'

'Well, I take it with thanks. Our places today shall be
on the cold ground; you can see furnitures are not of privy
to this place.' He looked up at the sky. 'Nor a roof. We
are not at the Holy Rood House, nor Bannockburn House
no more. Sadly. And there is a roof on St James's Palace,
where we should be sat at this moment.'

'Ah, come, sire. The way of these islands is to find
yourself in conference on the good earth, among noble
men who keep your cause – and none that it matters, as
God's will alone sent you to us.'

They both sat with crossed legs on the ground,

Clanranald upon his folded plaid, his fists clenched.

'Aye, sir, all sorts of fates powered me here.'

'I believe it, Your Majesty. Men come and men go, and they pass beneath, but you and your father carry a higher mission, sire; it's God's work about us here and we know it.'

'Well, I have never been so supported in my cause by such as you and your men. Your three regiments.'

Clanranald now looked around at the low stall. 'Were you to remain here, I would have all my best stuffed chairs taken from my house at Nunton this very eve and oared across directly to you in boats, for your better comfort.'

'Truly, sir, no need. We are off soon, and the rains would spoil such items.'

'I would accompany the chairs, gladly – and the oarsmen at task would endure a comfortable crossing, sat there on my soft chairs, in a strange formality for their heavy work.'

The Prince laughed, a little unsure if he was meant to, and looked at his knees. 'My arse has known worse. In the hills there, we were in the open roughlands after we supped with your Lord Lovat and abandoned our horses. We were billeted in more depleted circumstances. On snowy march in England, your men slept in open air, a hardship of the noble endeavour, but I am sorrowed I cannot offer you more.'

'Your Majesty, it is I who bear the sorrow, for the news that's been brought and still comes at this meddlesome predicament. But we can make providence work here for us.'

'We must. Well, all has gone to pot since Inverness, but I must cross to France to continue the enterprise, secure an army; soon, sir, I shall return the favour to this enemy. It only furthers my stance against Lord Murray and his collaborators that we never should have departed from out of England – we marched into Edinburgh, and I hold my ground that with one big battle we should have marched all into London town and lifted the crown from the ground where it would be resting, thrown aside in alarm.'

Clanranald bowed his head in answer to all this fine conjecture. 'Aye, Highness. To France for now it is, and this great price on your head confounds the hearts of rascally men. You must impress thought on trusting those around you. I turn all my powers to Your Majesty's predicaments, sire, for here, boats *are* power, and you will have learned the hostile Navy seeking you is to St Kilda. Sent and sailed.'

'St Kilda?'

'A distant isle.'

'And I am its king-to-be also? It is mine?'

'Of course, sire. Days' sailing and more for them to put ashore, where mad rumour was stoked that Your Royal Highness was in refuge; so the Navy ships is gone – a challenge for them to find St Kilda, conjoined with the sport of landing there when they anchor. It's a blasted place – an opportune moment to be seized. Sire, I want to present you with a masque and ball of my own invention.'

'A masque and ball, sir?'

'Yes, Your Majesty. Little moves here without my feathers ruffling, and I hear of a two-master brig on Lewis Isle for use. Should we take on Captain O'Sullivan to join the mischief, if it is your will, or we can talk alone?'

'Ah surely, Captain O'Sullivan. O'Sullivan?'

The Irishman ducked in immediately.

'Come and take a little council with us both, captain, for Clanranald wants to talk of masque and ball.'

'Oh? Speak more, sir, please.' O'Sullivan chuckled but elected to remain standing; then, feeling disrespectful, he slowly reclined on his haunches with his back against the rough wall. The Prince watched him, perhaps even a little envious of O'Sullivan's more comfortable-looking position.

'Captain. As His Royal Highness comprehends, at your disposal is a tutored crew of sailing men – there is a two-master you could obtain at price to take you directly to France with your capable boatmen, who I charged the idea with. The urge is on while the Navy dally over to the St Kildas. The Isle of Lewis is your place. Just to the north. Have your boatman MacLeod go to Stornoway – but take care. A beggar in Edinburgh can be a preening lord on this isle and be off to the enemy to undo you. My suggestion is a masque and tale you all join to, in fine performance. Say, sir, with your wisdom you chose a name, any name, and say you are all out of another place, the Orknies, with your ship faltered and in for repair on Tiree or Colonsay Isle. Because you have a differ in ages, use this by saying that you, captain, are in fact the blood father of His Royal Highness; and say you, Your Royal Highness, take a common name, any name, and adhere to this, and you can be the captain's son by name.'

The Prince spoke. 'Ah, a name to be bandied about like upon a theatre stage, but what name? What is to your fancy, Captain O'Sullivan, to be my new father?'

'I have always been a Sullivan and now I could make myself a Mac?'

Clanranald shook his head. 'No, no, captain. I would caution against the Highland names. You could trade for a steady Lowland title, Scottish, but denoting nothing in terms of what a name tells of us.'

O'Sullivan sounded as if in offence. 'But, sire, your name is everything and enriches us – a blessed thing.'

'It will be of less use if they snatch us through it. In this life, sometimes the tree is invisibled with the sun's rays placed behind. I can eclipse my royal and true name if all of us escape those marauders.'

'Mr Berrycloth!' O'Sullivan suddenly shouted out. 'I once met a Mr Berrycloth.'

'A fine name.' The Prince laughed. 'Mr Clodfankle?' he suggested. 'I heard the name in a theatre. Though I never met such a man.'

Clanranald laughed. 'Plainer fare is needed, I believe.'

'Such as?'

'Robertson is a solid Scots name which should throw no shadows. And what of this: Captain O'Sullivan claims as Mr Robertson; and you, sire, take a demotion in this world as his son, Mr John Robertson the Younger. Your destination will be the Isle of Lewis, saying the boat you sail now was from my brother, MacDonald of Boisdale. I suggest you make aim for the two-master and enable an agreement – but, Your Highness, captain, it is among the higher urgencies that no one has understanding of who is among your party, or alarms will be up. Set the riddle that you wish the brig immediately, but also set the fib that you want to return to your home, the far Orknies . . .'

'I have seen them mapped. Are they my lands too? Am I king-to-be of them also?'

'Well, of course, sire. These are all your islands around you, as sure as we sit on your ground now.'

'Good. Good. Continue.'

'Tell them of how you wish to gather a grand cargo of dry meal in the Orknies, so even in your inconveniences you are canny traders still, ready to turn coin, and this will justify your intent. For you will be required to pay real gold to obtain the brig. And, better, the busy tongues of the island will ignore the matter of your identities and sense gold to be made for themselves on your return. Thus, instead of making meditation on you, they will be off to anticipate these dry goods you return with. Meanwhile, under the dark of the first night of fair weather, ye shall be off under sail – not north, but south, for France.'

O'Sullivan and the Prince glanced at each other. The latter spoke. 'It's a sound reckoning, to my mind.'

O'Sullivan nodded slowly. 'We are to be Robertsons, it seems, sire.'

'Aye. But, MacLeod, who will make the purchase of the brig must be cautious.'

'Take sustenance, captain, from this.' The Prince was already chewing, and he held out yellow biscuit towards O'Sullivan, who rose, crossed and took the dainty. Both men devoured all the biscuit quickly, their mouths moving in silence and with no thought of sharing it with their faithful boatmen outside, any of whom could betray them in a moment for thirty thousand English pounds – an unthinkable jackpot.

∽∾∽

Later, when Clanranald had returned to his chairs on the other side of the island, O'Sullivan took the Prince aside and cautiously told him, 'This matter of new names, sire . . . I think Saint Clair – or, as they have it more, Sinclair – better than Robertson.'

'Sinclair, you say. But why, sir?'

'I trust Clanranald, of course I trust him, but what weighing of quality is there where a false name is a false name? Just conjecture: if someone is told in advancement somehow to watch for Robertsons who come not as what they are . . .?'

'You distrust Clanranald?'

'I distrust near all but you, sire. It is my duty to distrust. Forget Robertson. Let me be Old Sinclair, and you the younger, John Sinclair, and we will make a nice family scene. I have charged the men thus, and Father Macdonald will be a Mr Graham, a Highlander but not a man of the cloth.'

The Prince nodded. 'Let us make the voyage tonight.'

Chapter 4

In the mind of the Prince, all voyages were slowly to become as one tortuous voyage in his cankerous reckonings. The plan of the two-master for France, like all their plans, unravelled in days – the vessel was refused to MacLeod on suspicion. Again, the Prince and his wandering banditti were cast on to the open country of the isles, like foxes.

Through the month of May he rested for three weeks in the backlands of South Uist. No longer pale, but tanned in the face, bearded, and smoked as a kipper, in fair weathers he sat out of doors (though his cottage *had* no door) on a square heap of peat turfs cut by the men, formed into a mocking throne with armrests. Seated like some elfin lord of the forest, he smoked rough tobacco from a broken pipe, the stem repaired to inhale through using the

hollowed wing quill of a shot seabird. He was prince of
these sublime wastes, shores, bogs and lochans alone –
of six dirty shirts and his cottage, which he literally called
a 'palace'. And a prince with no more than this to deliver
unto his father. The escaper's progress was halted.

Given time for reflection, and gallons of brandy,
skittering in and out of depression and elation, he found in
his memories the terror of one boat crossing becoming
enmeshed with another, and then of more to come. They
accumulated so. In a manner, his existence was to be
defined by frantic voyages to and fro, hither and thither,
and there were to be instances, years and decades hence,
in palaces and by fountains, as silver goblets before him fell
from the tables onto marble floors, when all of these night
crossings and desperate daylight oarings, in their tellings
and retellings, recountings and narrations, would become
comingled, like sea water in oatmeal, charged with
whisky. Lying in soft feathered beds of real palaces – in the
Place des Vosges in Paris, or the Palazzo Muti in Rome –
he will sometimes awaken with that queasy, gelatinous
swell slowly slapping just beneath his back, only to realise
he is not supine in a small wooden boat on Scottish waters,
but is in fact safe, with the impress of perfumed female
company adjacent.

Unable to swim himself, he had learned to his
amazement that many of these coastal sailors could not
swim at all, and they considered a spill from a boat a

justified death for such grievous clumsiness, like a poor parry to a sword blow from a skilled combatant.

He became confused in these jumbled rememberings. For instance, the crossing over from what he called 'the continent' – by which he meant the mainland of Scotland – to the islands was, in legend, said to be in violent tempest, breaking the bowsprit. But that was not how he recalled it – all his life he remembered it as ominously calm, while he lay undone by seasickness. He recalled another, far more storm-lashed crossing. Strange how time fragments experience into splinters, passed between us all in words alone, in boasts, alarms and propagandas, until the truth itself is mere dispute.

With Donald MacLeod in considerable doubt about the weather, they had cast off northward for Lewis in their familiar boat, the oarsmen of the previous voyage in their places, and the pace seemed promising, the prospects deceptively fair. The Prince took up position near the bow, O'Sullivan at his side – and there they both stood, silhouetted against the fast-failing light, to take advantage of every moment of brief northern darkness, faces to the fore, the ominous breeze bothering their neckerchiefs, the lapels of their jackets, a supportive hand each onto the bare mast while they drove deeper, as the men lunged at the eight oars behind them. Father Macdonald, having adopted his assumed title, rested on the bottom of the boat towards the stern – uncommonly dry for now – splayed, as casual as if he were throwing dice on a drawing-room carpet. Behind him was the polished crossbench from where Donald operated the tiller. All of them besuited in what they considered ready appropriateness for the probable incursion of government raiding parties or search sorties. To be able to maintain they were not who they really were, under false names and purpose, beneath these tousy, alien skies – perhaps as all pass through this world, in delusion and deluding.

Like phantoms, then, these rash adventurers crossed between the islets in the new dark unknown, and longing to be unknown in their fugitive form, their continuance and survival was a matter of mystery given the odds, as if it really were God's will. If they were grabbed by this night on the waters, beneath the opaque surfaces of the depths, if all their eyes closed for that final time, who would ever have learned the final fate of these brigands, as each of their bodies were pulled to the base of the sea, as if on lines of firm cord, to be the food of crabs and crawling beasties without name? If the boat was capsized, and its heavy wood outweighed its fragile buoyancy, rather than be swept shoreward cleaned of its men, it too would have been slow-turned in the huge mixes of water towards the sandy bottom, where it would rest inverted like a slumped tent, soon silted over and rotted by the chemistries of decay always enacted upon things of the upper world now descended into the lightless places. Swords, dirks, the metal pot, pistols, muskets and coin would descend most swiftly – almost vertically. Perhaps only a single oar unjammed from its thole-pin would float and lap on the surface for many days, eventually berthing on a distant, lonely shore, to be bleached and harried by seasons until a wandering crofter collecting sea kelp in his rope-woven net bucket found that lance of wood, lodged by several winter storms between rocks; it would be carried on a shoulder to the sheiling, used to prop an outhouse corner, the unknown monument to their gloomy fate.

∽◦◦∽

'On the raft again, my dear father Sinclair? Is it not fine sailing weather to be on our way this night?' the Prince yelled from the bow, so the whole boat could hear – or at least the constituency of English speakers.

O'Sullivan smiled, called back to the jesting: 'Why, my good son John Sinclair, your kinship and company make it so. Is it not in our very bones to sail? For sailor folk like us, the ways are in our blood, being of fine Orkni Isles stock, born and bred to oar and sail.'

'Aye, my good father. It is your sturdy tutoring in seafaring ways from youth upward made me the bawdy salt fellow I am tonight. When in youthful disgrace as a child, you would ever slap my bared arse hard with a fish. Why, it is on the land alone I feel queasinesses galore. Here now is my born element. I take this air with joy; this sea is my sought-after paradise in all its form.' The Prince acted out a huge inhalation to his lungs so that he shook his head, then lifted a clenched fist skyward. 'I feel my loins invigorated moment by moment.'

'Yes, true son. It is in the blood of coastal traders such as we bear. And if I might caution you, does this invigoration account for your shoreside carousals with lassies high- and low-born, in notorious taverns and sites of infamy? Oh, John Sinclair, is it not true you are the terror of the lovers found in all ports? What is that toast you make so often to dark-eyed Frenchy princesses? You don't find such temptations in the teeming ports of Boulogne and Leith alone?'

The Prince grinned. 'Not in these waters. Oh no, my father. Don't scold in that manner so common to strict scions. The dark-eyed princess I toast comes from a nobility and a right of kings beyond your rank to question, Mr Sinclair.'

O'Sullivan looked a little chastened – yet risked his mocking jest more. 'But what of the lassies of Mull island, where once we were all bound from fair France? Is it not true that there you broke hearts aplenty, were pursued by fathers across valley-glens, far from your own chosen waters and boats? And then there was that wanton barmaid, a brown-haired lass of Oban, whom I learn you and the poets all celebrate – another set of dashing eyes on her, I believe?'

'More than eyes, dear father, more than dashing eyes.'

'Aye. I heard tell that you put a ton of dry wheat on the shore there, but more your true intention was fresh oats to put in, son of mine.'

'True. She was the dashing sort, Father. I confess, she could serve tavern whisky while sat upon your knee, and it was a shock when I calculated why she could not move from her place there in my lap, so firmly lodged upon me, as sure as this mast here in its fitting place . . . It is another strong defence of why we should wear the kilt at all times and not the affected trouser of the south, such a practical garment is the kilt in all ways.'

O'Sullivan guffawed. 'How your mother would lament, son. Another hungry bairn's mouth claiming your support.' He turned and cast an eye into the gloom of the boat. 'Attention there, Mr Graham. Mr Graham, do you hear this about my only son, John Sinclair – did you accompany my boy on this voyage of pleasures? I am only glad there is no man of the church aboard our vessel this eve to over-hear, only Mr Graham back there, another honest tradesman plying the portals of commerce, who would pass as a steady counter of coin . . .'

'What is that you say, Father? A cunter of coin, was it? Are you talking of the tavern maid again?'

O'Sullivan snorted with delight. 'Mr Graham would pass as a counter of coin – or such – to any naval officer of the withered Crown on these waters. Of it, I am sure.'

'Jest on, *Mr* Sinclair,' Father Macdonald shouted. 'Jest on with your terrible talk and, with my other true self, I will pray you are right when another John – John Bull of the Navy – stands before you.'

'Hear that, son of mine! We have a tender to prayer on board this eve – why, I thought he was a man of commerce, but he tends to the pampering of your soul, as well as rattles among those shoreside lassies.'

'Mr Graham is pure, but he would need a mighty prayer to cover all my straying, I fear, Father.'

'Well said, my only child.'

Ned laughed delightedly at his oar, and Father Macdonald shook his head. 'Don't join them in their daft play, Ned, my boy.'

'No, no. *You* are *my* boy. You are my boy.' O'Sullivan chuckled at the Prince, giving hearty slaps upon his shoulder.

'It's true, dear Papa, I am your boy, so defend me now from his judgements. For it was true love. Until she stood up and her skirts fell into place.'

The bow dipped into a swell and the boat lifted more.

Donald MacLeod shouted, 'All our judgements may be coming sooner than your reckonings, gentlemen. And if the two Mr Sinclairs to fore there might shout out in more useful voice when they see any big toasters rearing before us, I will have the boys lifting oars in good time. Row up the sides, and lift to go down any monster, lads, for pity's sake, please.'

O'Sullivan changed his tone of voice. 'Are we far out now, MacLeod? Is this the rolling of open seas?'

'It's the rolling of what I cannae see. I needs steer her straight up the slopes and go across the tops clean, never splayed. Put your eyes ahead of us, please, and shout if it seems we top a riser with the far side drop. Keep heaving, lads, we should have upped sail a while back; the wind is not aligned the ways I had reckoned. As I protested so onshore.'

The Prince and O'Sullivan fell silent in their games, glaring ahead onto the increasingly swelling surface, squinting, looking for that worst sign: a swell that begins to dissent and boil froth on the very summit of an unstable water mound. They both kneeled, fists on the foretop by the broken bowsprit stub, while the boat entered more of a sideways roll than formerly.

The Prince shouted out a rally: 'We shall manage all, my fine fellows, we shall manage, I assure you now. Chance is on our side. Heave, young Calum. See, men, he pulls to make me proud, as you all do. Young Murdoch MacLeod here stood with us by the Culloden House, out of school with five years and ten. There's Ned Burke heaving oar. You MacDonalds. Though I cannot quite see you. Never braver men – like the Greeks of ancient days, always at oar, I know you and your names. Tell those ones the same in Gaelic.'

The wind increased upon their faces within the swift hour, pushing their eyes into furrows of flesh. A vapour smoke blew off the razor ridges of the biggest tumblers that appeared out of the dark before them. The boat smacked down over the tops of these glens and spilled along the far sides, which became spoiled with frothing as the sea grew more demented by the wind. With an outright, grasping agitation, their craft shivered up further sides of water and every plank vibrated, drumming out the white caulking from between the curved boards. The Prince and O'Sullivan would turn from their pilot work – such as it was – 'A big one comes, a big one comes, row, row!' they screamed, and to keep up spirits even laughed together at their repeated dousings.

The fellows leaned to oars, desperate to power up the towers, and then they lifted oars in unison to drop into the repeating abysses below. MacLeod heaved at the tiller, often rising onto his feet to push with both arms at full deflection, keeping that bow straight for topping the ascent – as if they were on some fairground ride of the far future, into the billows and out of the troughs as they came.

Back waves terrorised them most, a glut spilling over the transom, so Father Macdonald was on his knees in the lapping basin of salt water, scraping frantically, cupping out handfuls across the sides until his fingers were lacerated and bleeding from the speed of his scooping and gouging at the boards.

The ocean pulled grimly at them. 'Should we haul sail-up, to speed from this?' Ned screamed.

MacLeod spat water from his face. 'Nay, nay. In rollers as these, you shorten any sail – any inch sail will coup us, for sure.'

'Is it doom, MacLeod? Is this to be our end? Give me knowledge of the end, so I can prepare myself. This is a cursed boat: it was the son of Borrodale's, who fell among us at Culloden House.'

Macleod spat again. 'Quiet yourself, Ned, it does nae good. Keep at the task. Captain O'Sullivan, please not to drop that pot over the side, or my wife will have me worse than any ending here.'

O'Sullivan had fallen to the bailing, angling the pot mouth into the accumulations and trying to tip it overboard without falling, or adding to the imbalances of the craft which so worried them.

The weather grew worse, the waters sizzling round about. Surely once they felt their low keel strike the bottom, or was it the shells and stones of the profundity, cast up in violence, hitting their undersides? What of the beasts of the sea – seals, whales and fish in all their forms – why wouldn't they circle this vessel and scream to be taken aboard, into a temporary sanctuary? How were they not smashed together and killed? The birds of the upper places in this turbulent air had ceased to fly, but the swimming things were helpless in choice of element. Maybe the sea was bloodied red in this darkness, with the massacres of eels and cod bashed together, their lippy mouths gasping up for air in an instant before they were sucked below?

Most of the rowers prayed aloud in Gaelic, an ululation to accompany the trickles of water down the inner sides of their hull, the crashing of the prow, the spills and torrents of peril about them.

Then, at last, they sensed a sudden change in the nature of the great floor beneath them. The swells lengthened in timing between each crisis. To gauge the coast, MacLeod lowered his chin strangely onto the gunwale, though each rocking placed his mouth almost level to the water's surface. He hauled the tiller and shouted in Gaelic. The rowing ceased, and two men rose – the sail man took the halyard, and the sail cloth ascended, cracked full, as the boat accelerated crazily ahead.

'We've cleared the head, sirs, but for God's sake watch to fore for the white of breakers and listen, listen with all your ears what we are coming in on. Silence those prayers, men. It is listening out for the breaking of waves ahead will save us, no praying – if we come in on rugged shore or cliff, we are undone, and will have to drop that sail and row to fight back out, try to come in leagues north. This we will only manage by luck as the wind is set. Pray for the light of dawn – but pray silently.' He repeated these instructions in hoarse voice, using Gaelic.

Nothing seemed to lie ahead of them, and the swell diminished, so MacLeod abandoned his haste, dropped sail and headed further north by oar alone, letting an hour pass as the elements calmed and the fear of inundation seemed less, until, with an infinite gentleness, the uprising of first light lifted a roiling roof of metallic cloud shapes above, then, shortly after, a long, low daub of higher ground showed to the west. They made directly inward to a thread of flat shoreline, born of that dawn with no knowledge of where the place was.

Chapter 5

On Corradale, young Neil MacEachain the schoolmaster had taken to spending all his time with the Prince. They had been hunting together since the darkness depleted, the Prince having commandeered one shortened gun. He had come from his cottage, and MacEachain from his sleeping place on a dried heather bed in the rough pantry.

In that frail light, which to weary eyes seemed to tremble, they walked some time without talking, stepping towards the Minch in that astonishing waste. By their sodden footwear, tall dew-soaked grass tufts tipped suddenly in soft breeze; the sightlines about them were immense. Over a lash of rippled water which moved, despite its illusory stillness, was a further fretted coast – or a universe of low coasts, placed one ahint another, as receding and jutting lochs confused the logic of the gaze. They had learned that what you saw among this mishmash of islands and flow lands was never apparent until you were just upon it; that the way ahead could resist passage due to a water channel, or that the risings hid coastal inlets; that seemingly horizontal land was a maze of small black baths reflecting the sky; that drops steepened and firmness underfoot became sucking bog with a single stride. Shortly, the two men were to be trapped on an island after being landed, leading to a hysterical fit of the Prince's, thinking himself marooned. Gradually, the tide was to recede, revealing an isthmus walkway to the main body of land, which they could walk across without even immersing their feet. They were used to this country, these Fata Morgana: all was mirage until you were upon it, as if continually moving into a new world of surprising immediacy, inventing itself in relation to your own arrival.

The inedible early birds, peewits or wagtails, shot up like sprung traps from their ground nests, and they hovered and screamed above; the two men lifted what eggs they found and selfishly ate them raw, immediately spitting shell shards from their lips, dapple-flecked convex, pearled inner concave. Herring gulls passed over low, curiously silent like possible informers, then tipped away. As if they had emerged from a cave, the western light was now translucent to them, and the brightening air was midge-free.

The Prince had shot two times at birds in flight, looking around himself and giggling – the flat phut of each powder discharge eaten by the dolorous spaces about, forging no echo from those green heights of Hecla or Beinn Mhòr, to their rear on this long island.

They were walking parallel to the shore and, with a near-vertical musket discharge that dislodged his bonnet, a gull had fallen like a stone bound in a handkerchief, but to the sea, too far out to retrieve as the currents tapped its broken white crescent wing further offshore.

The Prince shook his head, let out a groan. 'Heed, Neil, all flying fowl and winged things. What gift it must be to take to the wing at will and away.'

'You have had to take to the wing, sire – in an earthly way.'

'All too earthly.' He nodded. 'When we reach dry parlours, I will tip my head to the left and to the right for a month, and water shall leak from this ear on the carpets.' He mimicked tipping his ear to the left, tugging at the lobe and shaking his head with vigour. 'Oh, for a carpet.'

MacEachain laughed. 'Our clothes are overdue a drying fire.'

'Have you thought, Neil, how the fowl govern their unusual movements through the skies above us? Why go here, why there? Is it God's work in their dainty heads? Given wings, but despite having these abilities, some of these birds have chosen never to have departed this isle since they came from their *oeufs*? Yet sailors tell how some have crossed continents. Has a bird passed over our heads from a land a man has yet to walk upon?' He looked out at the water and frowned. 'I have fancy we are the first men to walk in many of these places.' He used his thumb to rub at the flintlock cap. 'When I was in the ducal states, the birds were a different affair. Many small things with no eating meat, what we called *uccellinos*. The *diamante de Gould*, the pecking *faisan* and that one . . . the name . . . but in French: *pintade*.'

'*Oui, monsieur, la pintade.*'

'As a child I was up at Gaeta, warring again, and there I would take note to the bird names in my *carnet*.' He considered Neil, while holding the short gun in an odd way, horizontal in both arms, as you would carry a sleeping child. 'I commanded artillery, but a child younger then than you now, do you know? As young as MacLeod's boy, Murdoch, but I commanded.'

'I am sure you did with commendation.'

He laughed sharply. 'I was a war-maker from youth.'

'I like to hear of these exploits, sire. Your most recent too, but, not being military, I also have a mind to hold my curiosities as conscience scolds me.'

'Why, Neil, ask of me as you please. Talking is always a cure for this foul hunger.'

'The excitements of war, sire – battles – they call to all young men. I don't want to talk of sore things. It is never for a curious fellow to ask you for scenes I only make in my own foolish head.'

'Aye, well. There were battles, for sure. You will have learned from my talk with MacDonald, Baleshere and others. And there will be more battles when the French come back to join with us in doubled force. But, Neil, take heed to have a steady nerve. When you see ball, cannon ball, move towards you from above, they come in slow then with damn haste in your close presence – they too are like black birds, but with a sting, a sting, for sure.' He took the gun in one hand, and with the other made a motion, an upturned parabola across the sky, taking in the shore, a phantom object advancing in on Neil then accelerating vastly.

'Yes, sire. Magnificent victories, though.'

'Not at that despicable skirmish on the Culloden parks before Inverness. What an upset. Ned Burke was there, my earlier companion, and the same Murdoch, Donald's boy, one of my oarsmen, who I talk with. Captain O'Sullivan on the retreat. But what a ruffle. Much better was a big fight we made on what they call the Glads Muir by Edinburgh, where we put them to flight around the walls, and another as we came out from the Bannockburn House and Stirling Castle's siege work, beyond the woods. In line order for two days and the start of a third, my army stood to tempt them onto us, General Hawley's mob, then we moved swift and caught them unformed at the place called Plein. Or closer to above Falk Kirk.'

'Gallant stuff, sire?'

'Men from these very isles put King George's ignorant to flight. Take no pride in such cruelties, though. You, young Neil, are a sprightly fellow of good mind. A university man. You will understand, this was both fair and sore to me, even the enemy who hunt us here today are my father's misled subjects. I called this out as many times on the bloody fields, to give them some mercy, but was not always heeded by my Highland men.'

'Are there blooded sights, sire? On the field, is blood as prominent as new rain?'

He laughed. 'Not so, but things remain beyond forgetting. I saw cannonade take a poor messenger in middle breast, and the ball carry him backwards until some of him went this way and some that, legs loosed and twirling like a stick you throw for the dogs. A lot of unnameable matter of him went upon the ground. His humours, spleen and heart, perhaps. Our forms are taken apart in horrid ways by the needs of it all. Beyond Plein, the enemy cavalry rode over their own to flee the top brae, and the foot ran for sport from the Highland men. The weather was filth yon day. In your rash Janvier, hard snow drops struck your eyes to close. Graupel. Often I thought the ball of muskets, or bones of men, had struck at my face, but it was your weather.' He laughed. 'The next day the stripped naked bodies of their dead lay up on the braesides like so many white sheep.'

'Men would thrill to stand on a field near your command then charge.'

The Prince spoke quietly. 'My Highlanders could be hard, Neil. Hard on the horses, I will remark. At Glads Muir I saw them attack riderless horses and bring them down cruelly. Being foot soldiers, they conceived of any horse as a beast which, once escaped riderless from the field, could hence return to them remounted and do equal mischief. Thus, they took off their forelegs and executed them on any opportunity at battle. At the hill beyond Plein and Torwoods, above the Falk Kirk, I saw the Atholls fall to the ground, let the horse go full over them and sword upwards into the bellies, to bring dragoons to ground. I comprehend they also saw all horses as property of the quality which they were helpless to profit from on campaign, so the instinct was to destroy. I tended to the rear – to the rear command, by custom – kept wracked by my fool Lord Murray, engineer of my misfortunes in some manner. I talked harshly of him to you the other morn. Murray was hard toil but steady. The Irish speak poorly of this man, and I have also, but this warrior had much to lose in coming out this year past, as he did in the 1715 rising; why would he do it just in order to betray me? It is an odd reckoning that we must do bad to do right justice. I have learned of the suffering of our people here at the hands of these government officers, and their raping, spoiling legions.' He raised his voice angrily, as if Ned were a culprit. 'Men nor do battles make kings, Ned. God makes kings alone, as he made these birds for our taking. The Almighty makes my own good father. This is why a wrongness was made with this King George, a failing in the fabric of my father's Godly right, and I am here to do justice for what the Almighty needs. The Holy Father speaks with me. Remember me to this. I saw my army go off for me and God, and I shook on my saddling, not with fear, but with fire to join them in this work.'

'You saw our pursuers put to flight as well.'

'Many times, many times, and we shall again.'

Neil laughed, a non-combatant's delighted, unlearned laugh.

'At Edinburgh, by Plein and through England, I had the resistor thrown aside. Though the filthy garrison at Edinburgh cannoned its own roofs from the castle, their balls reached not to Holy Rood. My palace. In England, bridges cleared and towns fell without musket discharge, by good sense of clever fellows. I can only understand that God wants to heighten the stakes to make the final justice so much sweeter, when the French come back and we take the crown, which we shall. I assure you, God is with me on that. I am his servant on this matter. These are all my father's lands, and I rightly claim them.' He stared out at the desolation, the shores and the birds. Which ignored him.

Neil nodded curtly.

The Prince turned aside and spoke no more, visibly

moved. They came together down a steep slope that forced them to rapidly scramble sideways, then their feet scattered broken seashell on a stony cove. To their right, another gull, dappled in its second winter feathers, tipped off a rock and flew, hugging the water where it was doubled in its turned-over reflection, but the Prince had not recharged his weapon and only stared at the bird. He stood still and slowly loaded. His face daubed with smoke soot as usual, now with black powder around his neat mouth – the lips of a sweet girl but for the rough beard.

A young black whale crossed the cove waters before them, bizarrely close in and putting the slow bulk of its curved spine clear above the surface with no noise, so initially both men had thought it a reef of dark rock revealed by a rogue swell – or surely just a large seal? Despite MacDonald of Baleshere's imprecations for silence in these hiding places, the Prince screamed, 'A monster, Neil, take heed, a monster from the deep, and enough flesh for a year!'

Neil was astonished at this manifestation so close to shore, and the more so as the short musket was shouldered by the Prince, who fired directly at the sea beast. The shot jingled up the water too short of the glistening flank, like a fist of casually thrown gravel. The man crouched and violently reloaded, abandoning the rod in his excitements as he ran further along the shoreline to keep pace with the leviathan. A piece of the heel on his shoe flew off. The whale seemed to come so close in to the rocky point that it must surely flounder there. It passed tight enough to the promontory; had they been so positioned, they could have hit its flank with a tossed stone. He fired again from his shoulder, but the shot must have travelled beyond as no strike was apparent.

He lowered the arm, let out a call of frustration in another language. The beast sounded and did not reappear. The slow coiling of the oily surface reconfigured to its former state.

'I cannot swim, Neil. Come for me and remove all of your clothing, if you please. Step from your breeches and all, and swim out and pull that terrible beast back in shore for us all. I cannot swim, boy.'

Neil stared at the Prince, meeting his eye momentarily. 'But, sire,' he whispered, then pointed, looking away from that demanding face. 'Sire, it does not die. It is gone. Into the profundities.'

'I tell you, I never miss. Disrobe fully at once and swim out, for its strength will be gone and it will come easy to your hand. Kick with all your strength.'

'Sire, don't ask this of me – the waters are fiercely chilled.'

'Remove your clothes! Not only would it invigorate me by example, it is a royal command. Swim!'

Neil glanced down then whispered, '*Vous vous trompez, la bête est vivante.*'

The Prince turned sharply from Neil and stared hard at that remorseless dividing line below the still sky: the surface of water, and the appalling unknown beneath the ominous slick, the divide where the air of life existed, and those ungoverned spheres below, where air did not.

After long moments, the Prince breathed less intently, nodded, his temper calming, and he looked Neil up and down in all his slim youth. 'Ach, you have the truth. It lives and travels on to cross the oceans. I could have had it, though. Tell no one of this moment, MacEachain. I hit a starling and I missed a *baleine* – it could be my epitaph in London.'

Chapter 6

My dear Marion,

*I have sent your daughter from this country, lest she should
be any way frightened with the troops lying here. She has
got one Betty Burke, an Irish girl, who, as she tells me, is a
good spinster. If her spinning pleases you, you may keep her
till she spins all her lint: or, if you have any wool to spin, you
may employ her. I have sent Neil MacEachain along with
your daughter and Betty Burke to take care of them.*

I am your dutiful husband,

HUGH MACDONALD

In darkest, moonless night, down from the shallow hill,
onto the hidden flatlands, came the Prince, Neil
MacEachain and Captain Felix O'Neil, through waves of
rain in their sleepless state. They had haplessly veered

again from the winding sheep paths in the darkness. The Prince thrust a foot out before him, as before — as ever — one foot after another foot, but he was still pulling the boot in the suck of the previous stride, as the rain tickled in his eyes and around his nostrils; more than any inclemency, this was the true irritation.

They stopped.

He had his baggage slung upon his back, impossible as it was to carry his fine pistols to hand, and what would be their use in such darkness? Not just damp powder. He could not see to shoot, and they could not see to shoot him. A body would need to come nose-to-nose in this dark rain and wind to discover its foe, to discover mutual presence, never mind duelling at paces. Paces had almost ceased to be — more lunges than paces — the lunges of proceeding cripples.

How would you know it was foe or friend without frank discussion? And in this dark, how would he be discovered? Using Gaelic, MacEachain would claim to be a sheep herder in the dark, and they would bid one another a Samaritan's goodnight, before each passing on. The Prince, MacEachain and O'Neil needed to call out to find one another, moving in an ant-line. Sometimes MacEachain followed behind him, clinging on to the back of the Prince's slung baggages, and O'Neil placed a hand on MacEachain's shoulder, like blind beggar men in a candle-less night church, come in procession for alms.

The way to have peace on this earth: blindness for all. For sightless men could make no war. It would take armies of the unsighted for peace to be; one week of shouting to form into battle line, their slaughtering diminished into a tribe of the enfeebled. No arguments, then, about who takes the right flank. For where *is* the right flank and where the left? The whole army calling one to another in terms of detachment and formation. From reveille to night sentries, infinite babble. Formation in a formless void. When is it night to the sightless? Calling to the enemy across the parks of darkness with their separating distances, *We are here; are you there? Yes, but you stand at right angles in flank to us – straighten up, straighten up. Call to us, please, call to us, and face us, so we can begin to shoot at you, in about one week more. The cannon? Are you certain our cannon face them, and not us?*

'Neil, my shoe is lost again. Hold up, if you would be so good.' They stopped. He turned and felt at MacEachain's body, using it as a signal post to move his palms down towards the youth's pale feet. The Prince knew his own shoe must be sunk somewhere forward of the cold bare toes of Neil; for Neil was now walking unshod in these prodigious rains, through the night bogs. The left and the right turns they had taken to regain the better ground, up through the quagmires. The Prince was too cautious to go bare-footed like a farm boy, to cut or blister up his heels, for mobility was his only possibility of saviour. The Prince knelt before Neil, and it was the same performance: 'But, Neil, I cannot find the thing.' MacEachain smiled grimly and stooped once more, his fingers in bog water and myrtle, the cold, as he dug at the muck, locating and forcing up the footwear slowly free from the gruel, like peeling out the rib bone from the flesh of broiled meat. 'Ah. Here it is, sire.'

'Ach, Neil, I am minded to give up the ghost, and us lay together for warmth in our plaids till dawn light.'

Captain Felix O'Neil shouted from behind, 'We have to go on, sire, we must go on now, we cannot embrace quilting-up yet. We must achieve Rossinish, the clear beach to its north, to find these ladies and our exit point.'

The Prince sighed, rose to his full height, felt for MacEachain's cheek and jaw before putting a hand onto his shoulder to balance on one foot and wedge his footwear back on. The boot was like a liquified putrescence, melted by some heat apocalypse. The leather hide was straight, meaning it mattered not what shoe was placed on the left foot or what on right, which was of practical use when both were simultaneously seized by the mud, and the pair tugged and slurped free together. He spoke out in the dark. 'Have we ever struggled so severely to make the acquaintance of two handsome ladies on any night before this, my gentlemen?' MacEachain and O'Neil had to chuckle aloud. 'For it must be promise of a mightily romantic rendezvous for such penance as this.'

But O'Neil coughed, signalling he was a little discomfited at the rude jest, a little holy around the topic of Miss Flora: twenty-four years, unmarried with black eyes and well familied, having MacDonald of Armadale as her stepfather.

❧❧❧

So, on they went through the obscurities, dragging their bodies ahead. Forward, northward they came to the borders of Rossinish at the midnight hour itself, close to the shore and the shieling they were to meet at, but not the embarkation cove itself, which was better hidden even further north. They heard the breakers on the shingles with no visible feature to mark it. MacEachain went ahead, alone, to seek the shieling, instructing O'Neil and the Prince that, despite lack of sanctuary from the elements, he would never discover them on a solitary return to a featureless bog, so they must take themselves to lie upon the rough shore there. Thus, without shouting aloud, he would come upon them efficiently by following the line directly along.

In the rain, O'Neil and the Prince sat waiting, receiving wet on top of wet, until within the hour MacEachain returned out of the dark, accompanied – as far as could be made out – by a starved-looking urchin boy, who clung to

Neil's sleeve to prevent their separation. In low voice, MacEachain spoke. 'We find matters not as we would wish, sire. Flora and the Lady Clan are not with us as yet, and worse, twenty or so militia are tented hard by. This lad of the shieling will show us a modest bothy not far distant, for this night at least.'

'In God's name, I am undone once more by you all. God's name. Undone, MacEachain. Damn this, and damn you all.'

At the outburst, the child retreated behind MacEachain.

'They will take me with certainty, and what prize. *Baiser une truie!* Christ! Here, man, here, waste no time hanging me first.' The Prince knocked his fist hard onto his breast then fumbled in the wet shirt that stuck to his chest, tugging the fabric from his breastbone using thumb and forefinger. 'Take one of the dirks this moment and break in through these bones to gouge out my heart, burn it before my living eyes – huh, if you could strike fire in this filth. For in London town, after a farce of judgement, this is my fate, after our glories – hung, drawn and quartered, butchered like a young sow.' He shouted, 'Or worse, placed in confinements and, by stage, poisoned in my food month-on-month, so it can be said that my weakened self declined in confinement and my supporters have no execution to high martyr me upon.'

'God's sake, Highness, lower your voice, please. *Silence, s'il vous plaît.* This enemy could be open to our cause, but there is as good odds they have a Southerner amongst their lot.'

MacEachain and O'Neil both tried to assure him that Miss Flora and the Lady Clan would not fail him, though the Prince mumbled to himself frequently in Italian, as if in high fever. The child led the trio on through the blackout to that alternative bothy, which was not so very distant – though this in itself was a matter of unease with enemy so close.

There, in their inundated accoutrements, they put out into the rain a solitary sheltering cow; and through all remaining night hours, the clod roof sweated abundant drops, as if a large cistern was debouching above them. The Prince spat out only one demoralised sentence: 'It washes away some of this muck upon us at least, my fellows, it washes away the muck at least.'

At dawn light, O'Neil became cognisant that he had slept the night upon a softened cow pat. The rain and moving mist was ceaseless; small individual clouds rolled across the moorland like wagons. The Prince, thumped by insomnia, impatient in a manner never displayed before, tried to persuade MacEachain to cross the isle to Nunton House, for fresh informations on the two ladies – had they

perhaps been taken? MacEachain demurred: 'I myself
cannot leave you, for danger is real and close by. Neither
you nor Captain O'Neil can manage well at length in the
Gaelic – a situation could arise of misunderstanding, and
we must spread a convincing falsity of our true selves
often. The tale we spun of us as Irishmen seeking passage
home was fine diversion before, and we should repeat it in
all instances when credible; if a misunderstanding got afoot
in talking without Gaelic to the people of this place, it
could divulge up Your Highness to them. These militia are
everywhere.'

'I shall go. I shall go for you, sire.' Captain O'Neil
stood. 'You know I would lay down myself to you, sire. If
I am taken, it is as a lone Irish fugitive, and they will wring
no knowledge from me until the end of time. Let me go
for you; in daylight it will be as a dance compared to our
meanders of the night.'

They watched O'Neil, with his small knapsack, move
away into the bog network until he was gone in the cloud.

'Mr MacEachain, now do you believe, as well as
serving against my own undeniable hazards, good Captain
O'Neil might also be as fresh to see Miss Flora again?'

'Aye, well. There might be a wee flickering light there,
sire. You deduce correctly, I think.'

The Prince chuckled. 'Well, she comes as a bonnie,
bonnie lass – but, Mr MacEachain, I think she inclines
somewhat towards yourself.'

'Hush, sire.'

'Why, you blush, Neil. Don't be so churchy at a snapping lass like yon.'

And he would have gone ahead teasing, but they both ducked in alarm as two distant figures approached on the shoreline; however, it was now the child and his own mother, the cow-herder from the shieling – as Neil had warned, speaking in the Gaelic alone. They revealed that the militia rose late, but in the mornings they came to them for milk, and even this secondary bothy was too exposed.

Being so warned and then left, the Prince and MacEachain crouched and moved down onto the only hiding place which existed, the open shoreline, where they found a low boulder to shield them from any landward observation. On its seaward side was a slight concave indentation worn from erosion. They also had to consider possible sightings from passing boats, and in mind of this, into that evil declivity the Prince rammed himself, among the barnacles, urchins, limpets and leathery straps of seaweed, with which they would drape themselves in watery camouflage from any seaborne watchers, should they pass.

Though MacEachain reclined in the full open, the rock's dimensions failed to protect the Prince from the vertical rain which poured down. He lodged and clung in there, in this element of seeping liquids, as if he too was some troubled mermaid, crawled from the seas to birth a glistening spawn jelly ashore.

After some hours in such monotonies, the deluge eased then fully ceased, and the juddering wind too had depleted, but here arose in wafts of mild air swarms of violent midges that coated their faces and hands; they both had to motion ceaselessly, as if soaping themselves in a constant ablution, one hand rubbing the other hand, then both palms furiously slapping the face, like beings afflicted with a deranging tic, and acknowledge that man is not made for this open world, that we come upon the wide earth as strangers not adapted to its nature – indeed, it is our enemy.

Close by, a crab moved in a series of rapid advances and halts, and the Prince grabbed for it, but missed, before it scuttled back into water. With envy, they thought of the armoured crab and watched seabirds on the wing, which moved through the air unmolested by these infernal mosquitoes. Pocket the hands, but then the face is attacked; their neckerchiefs, ill-suited as face-masks, slipped from brows in their wetness, while the midges penetrated their hair and fed on their scalps.

'Oh my God, Neil, I would as soon walk to the militia and surrender myself up as take this plague for one hour more. These minute demons cause torments beyond their dimensions, an invisible foe. Do you think, Neil, your Lord put some creatures on the earth, and the Devil himself some others, to perish us? Was this debated at your seminary? The strawberry and the yellow honeybee come from God's handiwork, the barbed stinging hornet and the louse of the itch from the Devil? I am of the opinion there was a fighting factory on the day of Creation, for why bother with these? Curious thought. Yet men swarm the peopled earth too, in our vanities and cities; we seek blood also like these floating termites.'

They scratched and fidgeted until MacEachain and the Prince checked the whole horizon, crawled on all fours to the sea edge and baptised their entire heads into the salt waves, in search of relief, but after shaking the water clear, in minutes, the swarms were upon them again.

Yet some hope was offered after midday. The child from the shieling came running on the shoreline to tell MacEachain that the militia men had upped tent and departed. So, they were formally led to their destination, the Prince walking at fair pace ahead, the child having to trot to keep up.

In daytime, the cow-herd mother of the shieling seemed younger, perhaps even handsome, with her tight collected hair fixed by bone combs back from the face, the cloths bound hard across her small breast, her skirting of rough cloth, stained but slight, for practicalities of movement with no aproning. Her eyes were clear and young, but lines at the side of her face from a toilsome life gave her no certain age between twenty-five and thirty-five. The Prince considered her thoughtfully, his steady countenance always cautious of betrayal in recent days.

'Put the elder child to watch for comers.'

'He is out and at it,' replied MacEachain.

'How many bairns has she?'

'Three, sire, the two younger in the back room.'

'Three at her youth, such as it is? She takes pleasure in seeking after abundancy. Where is her man? Was he out with us in the rising?'

'No, sire, he has been taken to Barra Isle, for his brother is sick there and it is probable he is unable to return, what with troops demanding passage letters.'

'Hmm. What if he does return and takes alarm at us here with her? Presumes she has taken not one, but two hearty lovers, on her all day as she so loves the act?'

'Sire, please. He is gone a while, and like she, both are trusted by the MacDonalds.'

'Hmm. Were the militias fair to her? They did not try to use her, or paw her, in any particular foul way? For she has a frowsome spirit about her figure, her eyes.'

'No, sire, there were her own people among them, and they took only milk.'

'What food has she here?'

'None this day but cow milk for the bairns; she was to

be away for balls of meal from a neighbour, but the troops feared her to leave the elder bairns for a half-day. She has no knowledge who you are, sire, but an Irish officer. It's better this way, at all times.'

They were welcomed in, and the Prince greeted her inside the poor shieling cottage with his halting, oddly pronounced Gaelic, and she bowed. He made straight for the new fire in the corner where he sat on a stool, seemingly in a trance, oblivious to all but the pleasing heat. At his side, the woman bent and busied herself, adding more peat clumps, and she hung a bowl then crossed to the crowded corner of chattels, where she dumbly stood.

Suddenly, to the settled eyes of the woman, the Prince said, 'I must dry my clothes; tell her to be as accepting as if she were a good campaign-wife; she need not go outside or to the bairns.' He began to remove his wet clothing – every garment – so for shame, the woman looked aside, increasingly alarmed. MacEachain reassured her. Finally, the Prince was clad only in his damp shirt, which fell like a night gown upon his thin thighs – to offer some little modesty. He bent, revealingly, to place his mud-clagged boots up close to the fire's edge, so that they soon smoked like two steaming clods of fresh animal dung on a cold day. Sitting on the stool, like a strange fisherman at catch, he used kindle branches to dangle in turn his stockings, breeches, then jacket and trousers, by the hot orange light of the peat, a coiling steam slowly marauding upward off

their surfaces as he turned them at angles. 'Is there
anything to eat yet?'

MacEachain smiled, and in ironic voice stated, 'Here,
sire, see here. She now offers you her finest thick cream,
from the most noble of their wide herds, fed on the rich
grasses of springtime – the best cream you will taste in
Scotland, I would believe.'

The fevered man missed every tone of the ironic jest
and quickly took the bowl of watery hot milk, with a
horned bone spoon, from the woman; without thanking
her, he thrust the spoon and much of his filthy hand deep
into the wooden dish, anticipating lifting a mighty glut of
luscious white slime to his lips. Instead, he screamed and
cast the bowl and spoon aside, so both clattered on the
hearth then fell to the hard mud floor, the liquid hissing
back from the fire like a furious, roused tomcat. '*Putain de
merde!*' He flew to his feet, his shirt leaping up and down
to wild effect, shaking his right hand and looking at it.
'*Putain de merde*, she assassinates me – this witch is a spy.
Christ!' He shook the hand more. 'What do you set upon
me now, man? It is a scalding soup.'

'Sire, I was a-jesting. Pardon me, I was jesting, for it is
such meagre fare. It is yesterday's cow milk.'

'Keep your culinary jests in such desperate hours, man,
are you madder than I?' He turned on the woman. 'Rustic
fool, despite your form, that you should trick me like this.'

'It was I, sire, not she.'

'She is witch and traitor enmeshed; why, she should be goodly lashed for it.' He licked at the back of his hand. 'Lashed good and efficiently, with duration.'

MacEachain spoke harshly to the woman who, terrified, had retreated further into the chattel corner, looking at the floor.

'Strike her one *souffler*, Neil, and strike her good.'

MacEachain looked around. 'Not with my bare hand, sire, surely? With what?'

'You are a schoolmaster, so stroke her steady and severely as one of your errant pupils.'

Neil MacEachain looked around him. 'There is the leather of your money pouch belting, sire.'

'No, leave that. It dries.'

MacEachain crossed to the corner, urging the woman aside, and he crashed items akimbo, some which fell to the ground. He lifted the most exaggerated object that came to hand: a short wooden paddle, not an oar, a coracle paddle. A bairn began to scream in the back room at all this cacophony.

The Prince sat down again on the three-legged stool, watching. 'A worthy administrator, but it should be used exclusively on her flesh rump, such as it is, not upon her upper self. We are not brutes of men.' He stared at the woman. 'On her rear end there with the skirting, such as it is, pulled fast on that part by her hands alone, so the insulation of each blow is made minimum, and she feels the full biting knowledge of her crime, and it is set a-ringing there, hot and true, for the day long, to remind constantly of me. Put her to recline her frontage across that table and expose the fine target, as one dozen sharp blows are severely delivered. She should be so willing, and it would bring a fine sense of order to her.' He paused. 'Were such punishment ever to be carried out, it would remind her. Were it ever to be carried out. Ach. Threaten her with the deed alone, Neil, and let us forget the thing. I am merciful. My humour is poor today, I confess to it.'

'Are you sure, sire? Is the hand injured?'

'No, no, please, now. I reverse my battle orders; I commute the sentence. Leave her be. Leave her be. Woman, woman.' He slung his arm at her. 'Drop your alarm. Tell her. Go to that vexed bairn and bring it me here, I want to see it. It would calm me.'

MacEachain put the paddle down, crossed to the woman, who flinched, and he spoke seriously but with low voice in their language, explaining that his master was a good man who was overlooking her misstep; that he was sore harried, not by ill nature, but from battle scars which were not upon his body, but upon his mind, for a brave Irish fighting officer at the front of line in fierce battle sees pain everywhere around him, and is in association of this danger, which he expects at all times; this hot food had transported him into that injured condition for a few moments only, so he took such immediate offence, but now his condition was tempered to what it should be.

The woman, clearly traumatised, slowly brought back a crying bairn in arms from the rear room to the near-naked Prince. The man's nature had utterly transformed, and he stood, gently touching aside the poor swaddling to see the child's eyes, and remarkably, the child fell silent at his scarred, muddied countenance. In leery fascination, the Prince complimented the woman repeatedly on her child, and he kissed the very injured hand then bestowed royal blessing on the now-silent babe's brow, commencing a steady translation of praise, through MacEachain, upon her child's name, its vigour, fair cheeks and her mothering prowess, asking after its age and appetite. The Prince sharply retreated from this line of enquiry soon enough as MacEachain translated details of why feeding from the breast no longer continued et cetera.

Later, he softly asked her for bedding so he might recline alone by the fire's heat. It was swiftly brought, and it was another torn sail, so vintage and pandered by coastal breezes as to be soft as linen.

The Prince slept by the fire, far into the afternoon, with his overcoat as pillow, wrapped up like a slim mast, while MacEachain dried his own outer clothes, draped in his plaid, then dressed. He talked quietly with the mother and bairns in the back room; they discussed figures of the community known to them both, and their varied

worthiness, trying to keep near silence, until the urchin
came sneaking indoors to warn of a distant figure
approaching. This threw both men into new alarms, and
the Prince rose in disarray, dressed himself frantically and
made to exit from the shieling with such haste that he was
in shirt and opened waistcoat alone, his dried long-coat
jacket was loose, simply swung over his shoulder in his
hand, along with his baggage sack.

But this figure approaching was only a guide, named
Porro-Dan, from Nunton come, bearing gifts in sacking: a
cooked fowl and two bottles of wine from the Lady Clan
herself, with news that the plan proceeded. The Prince
was now delighted, and he stamped his boots in a mad
little dance, shedding dried soil onto the floor. The elder
child laughed with him, and the Prince enthused to hear
that the militias had cleared from this end of the island.

The tacksman was sent off with relevant messages, then
the fowl and wine were hastily consumed, the men tearing
the meat with their fingers and sucking clean the bones, the
Prince especially swigging jock-fellow-like from the bottle-
ends. His fair humour was hugely elevated. The scraps
accumulated in the sacking, and some of a single wing, were
presented up to mother and urchin, and she was even
invited to sit relatively close by him, but on his left side. The
Prince took great pleasure, smiling, observing her and her
urchin together, gnawing at the fare. 'Look, MacEachain.
Why, earlier today I was to review her sound thrashing, yet

now she eats by my side, and knows not she sits with one who has dined with kings of Europe. What a jumbled conjunction you come by in this strange world. Is it not so?'

∽✑✑✑✑

Despite his high spirits, with the rain gone, the Prince insisted they should sleep night itself again under open skies. More cautious than the risker of old, he feared that the upturn in his fortunes could be directly reversed by some rogue patrol, so he took dry swaddling rag for his face against the midges. He and MacEachain made towards the lower elevations of heather they had come down from in the ghastly night, and when the loss of light halted them, they found a good cleft in the peat rims to be hidden among, come dawn. MacEachain ripped up a bed of heather for their upper halves, and they wrapped in plaid to sleep side by side.

At dawn they climbed higher, and there settled for the day's watch, to keep sentinel for any approach of the Lady Clan, Miss Flora, and their potential entourage – or other more disquieting movements upon this earth and water. But it was a day in utter vain, for not a thing moved upon the lands spread around them, from coast to coast. There was a middling and current breeze, which kept what the Prince called 'the terror mitches' away.

In an unguarded moment, the Prince talked of a fine lady who had cared for him at Bannockburn House, in January month, when he was taken with a savage grippe, whom he named as Clementina, or Clemmy Walkingshaw, possessor of innumerable charms and huge gentility. 'Walkingshaw, and verily I walked directly in,' as he boastingly put it to his male companion. Then he became quite poetic in talking of the mysteries of grace found in high women, their mercurial natures and passions, and how this woman revealed 'hot surprises and revelations', about which he found it impossible to fathom by what manner she could have come by such proclivities and wily instincts. This again, as was his habit of reasoning, he could but put down to motions and operations of a divine nature alone – for there was no other possible explanation. Other than – he speculated – this woman was driven by the power and influence of moonlight, for she seemed to take pleasure in bathing in it, and was it not possible that the moon which wheeled about the warmed chambers of Bannockburn House at January night, driving its full bars through one window and out the other in their upper floors, might have also communicated some lunar essence unknown to men but receivable only by women, as with the sea tides – as it is known the moon influences their revolving calendars of curse and procreation?

Neil asked if that was not aired with a tint of heresy, more than considerations of science.

'Heresy, no.' The Prince laughed and added obscurely that, in his experience, women worked their way back from childbirth, a gift-skill in all of them, from pauper to princess, and that they operated with endless pocketfuls of unexplainable instincts and swift fiery abilities, which are a delight to witness suddenly revealed. In his opinion, they could be the wiser sex by far, for men seemed doomed to learn by experience alone, and not instincts, which are lodged in women innately.

∽∽∽

They suffered yet another night in the open, but with first light, and by straining their eyes in unison, they were sure a small boat moved round upper Rossinish, and within an hour, two tiny, clear figures came along the sheep paths towards the distant shieling.

They both descended cautiously, with prepared alibis, but as they approached the rough fanks, the Prince was elated with joy. 'Why, my God, it's two good MacDonalds, my previous oarsmen from first crossing here.'

Standing with the cow-herd mother and elder child were John and Roderick MacDonald, who had rowed with the Prince and Donald MacLeod those months before, and who had heaved him through the dangers to Stornoway. The Prince did not embrace the brothers, but he fairly

shook both their hands, long and heartily, though he
revealed he had forgotten their forenames; but it mattered
little, and they spoke a good deal of the English. They
asked after Captain O'Sullivan, and if he might have
perished, both it seemed out of rugged affection and
genuine curiosity for the man – as, to their knowledge, the
militias had failed to stir this Irishman out. Roused to
laughter, the Prince explained with sincere feeling that the
captain and he had parted with tears on both their cheeks,
to meet again in France. He laughed the more so when the
two brothers explained they too had been serving with the
militia, to take its penny, but had worked against the
discovery of the Prince or indeed any fugitives; they had
ignored figures on hills, been lax in checking passports and
letters of passage, and in the execution of all orders, to the
edge of mutiny – when no officer was in their sight. But
greater joy than this, these two men brought direct
instruction that MacEachain was to now cross on patrol to
Nunton and bring back the suitable boat with Flora, and
the Lady Clan, round the top of the isle, through the
narrow organ of water there, to their current place for a
crossing to Skye Island, as previously mooted. These two
brothers would again row their Prince, they told him.
MacEachain was off directly, and the MacDonald brothers
unveiled gralloched meat, of an ox or lamb, to feast
on later.

Chapter 7

That evening – finally confident the approaching craft was friendly – the Prince and the two MacDonald brothers came out of their skulk in the brush, fully down the foreshore, to stand at water's edge; they watched while the eighteen-foot, one-mast shallop moved along parallel to them.

'A dainty vessel,' the Prince quietly remarked, perhaps haplessly thinking aloud.

'But swift for you, sire, aye, sound enough come this crossing, and sure – we have used her before. Two rowers more who come.'

'Forgive, I am a wee bit saucy and spoiled still from the frigate *Du Teillay*. Five hours good pounding – continual fire, musket, then cannon – off the French coast, between an HMS man-o'-war and our own, *Elizabeth*. I never

comprehended ships lay so close together when they fired
on one another. What a sight, sirs. Sixty-eight guns, seven
hundred men. After *Elizabeth* was ruddled up very poorly,
I ordered my *Du Teillay* away onward, and we were
carried two weeks to your isles here, under – I mind his
name fine, as I now know yours – a Captain Darbe. No
lights at night, save a wee lantern sometimes lifted for the
compass. On *Du Teillay*, when we lay anchor by Arisaig the
year last, we had a tenting up on deck, like as to a campaign
tent, with brazier, bread and wines, for this relieved my
seasickness, to be in open air and not lodged below. It was
not a huge ship, a frigate, but spry and I have hopes the *Du
Teillay* shall return for me. All this could account for my
disorder when we crossed first together with Mr MacLeod.
My poor education then was such that boats of this
dimension' – and he indicated the shallop passing off the
shore – 'were for after-dinner diversions on the ornamented
lakes of grand châteaux, and now I am better informed.'

The two brothers marvelled at these many wonderous
tales coming off the Prince, and their casual reporting by
him, he who liked to stand at a certain angle, his arm
canted by his side while he recounted them, always a
gentle smile just arising, as if cheekily testing the brothers'
limits of credulity.

'Aye, well, sire, we will be lacking much of a tent
aboard yon, but for an English umbrella if Miss Flora
brought one.'

And all three of them waved their arms in friendly greeting, for there aboard the small rowing boat was the seated figure of schoolmaster MacEachain himself, returned at oar; Angus MacDonald held the other, there was the Lady Clan herself, with her seven-year-old daughter, wee Peggy, also Angus's wife and his sister, Miss Flora. Of course, next to Flora in the boat, reposed an attentive Captain Felix O'Neil, his wide-set blue eyes roaming.

All the women sat in column, hoods and caps affixed erect, in a strangely still and eerie tableau, like a mute funeral party come aboard a death boat to mourn among some stricken and grieving congregation. The shallop slowly passed abeam, to take account of tidal currents, then it pointed round to return and bear accurately in onshore. The men called huzzahs, and the vessel beached with its bow driven well up the dry shingle.

Angus, followed by MacEachain, jumped ashore, assisting the ladies down onto the dry shingle, the Lady Clan first, as she swung her skirts off the bow then stood.

Taking her, and despite his none-too-clean face, placing a French-style kiss to both sides, as was his custom – often with men as well as women – the Prince laughed and said, 'You will predict the happiness with which I see you once again, madam.'

The Lady Clan seemed of such high excitements she hardly addressed the Prince in any formal way, but spoke breathlessly, as if to an old friend. 'Excuse this parade.

I have grabbed here many examples of the family, for we thought it a more explicable presentation to these cursed invaders that we were boating round to visit a weak, sick child not to be long of this earth. So, I loaded us womenfolk especially, in good number, to douse suspicions.'

The Prince laughed more. 'But I am joyed at your whole viewing party. Come along with me, madam, we prepare the evening meal,' and after greeting all the others with a bow and thanks to them, he took the Lady Clan's arm to move up the beach, linked together, as if they were preparing to enter an opera house.

That small platoon followed to the shieling bothy, so there was quite an aggregation within. The Prince himself, assisted by the MacDonalds, placed dunks and clobbers of meat, the livers and hearts of beasts, on metal lines, and they were fried up good and served to all, piled pell-mell in a wide old crockery; wine too had been brought from Nunton, which the Prince was into, with a good few hearty-go-downs; bread and cheese, fresh milk too appeared – so all was jolly, with even the cautious sheiling wifie present, until the runner Porro-Dan came abruptly to the door and spoke in Gaelic.

The Prince sobered, stood attentively, ceased his joking and playing with the wee daughter, Peggy. Articles and baggage were hurriedly gathered while MacEachain explained, to the horror of the English speakers, that a thousand troops at least had arrived on the other side of the island, and they were patrolling once more. After the Prince quickly gave a single, generous coin to the shieling wifie for her many distresses, they were all off and away yet again, overloading the boat, the crockery of uneaten meat also, which the Prince carried in his lap. He sat on the bottom, leaning against the gunwale, like a lost and humble server searching some elusive banquet.

All the party escaped afloat down the Loch Usquebaugh, a tricky row, keeping well inshore, to an even more desolate locale on tougher berthing – a rough bothy shelter, fitted only for summer grazing. Nevertheless, the Prince insisted once the party was ashore in that place that they continue their supper, but they could not risk a night fire, so the cold meat was distributed with wine, as a strange breakfast, it being around five, before light.

Now, by foot at dawn, came a man called Donald and another man named Mr MacMerry, who were to be auxiliary rowers, both trusted tenants and workers of Clanranald.

Despite the further grave news which they carried, the Prince later spoke to them, saying, 'A fine name, Mr MacMerry, and I hope you come ready with some merry jests for me on our coming wee voyage.' MacEachain observed how, when meeting any person of high or low station – a great chief of eight hundred fighting men, a general, a beggar or an orra man – the Prince, without fail, held a necessity to impose a striking and always pleasing impression of his easy humour. A man who though so capable of it, he came with only bursts of hauteur, and surely one day as king this would make him a truly great one, he who had passed among so well and was so knowing of every form of his Scottish peoples?

MacMerry explained to the Lady Clan that the Captain Fergusson of HMS *Furness* landed close to Nunton House itself. In English, MacMerry informed her, 'They are fully established. The captain slept in your ladyship's own bed last night.'

'How quite disgusting, in every way. I will ensure fresh linen on my return. If our house still stands.'

'There is also a substantial party of troops under the General Campbell, a good man, but the same who took our Mr MacLeod. All told, close to two thousand red-coats strong.'

The Prince spoke. 'Would they put your roof to fire, madam, please not?'

'They have so many houses, high and low.'

The Prince fell to a heavy silence on this then urged that she return immediately with her young daughter while it was early daylight.

'I must, sire, and in my pleading to these invaders, perhaps my husband and I can save properties and livestocks, or they will be sacked most awfully, and my people put on the hills. If I return with the others here, our story of "husband-at-home, but I visiting stricken child" will still stand us good, for why would I patrol my daughter-in-law and young daughter on a mission across wild country to assist you? Sense says I would travel light. Let me add, the price of safety for Your Royal Highness stands above all else.'

'I comprehend this, madam,' were the words spoken, 'yet know you have transcended your duty long ago in all you have done for me, and your family's reward will be notable when I return with the French to make my father king. Go, madam, with your daughter and others, go and give my obligation to your husband for all this past year, and we will be away ourselves come first darkness.'

'Flora' – the Lady Clan turned to the young woman – 'all things lie with you for our family. You hold the passport letter, so initiate the intentions with care. All you need is here in the wrappings.'

The majority party rushed inland with curt farewells, and this left only the essential crew.

Captain Felix O'Neil remained by the Prince though, and standing beside Miss Flora, said, 'I despair at the earliness of the day, for we must be at sea already to ensure escape, and we cannot afford to sail before nightfall.'

It was then that Miss Flora displayed the folded letter of passport and told O'Neil, 'But, captain, I fear our numbers must be diminished yet – look at this passport. It mentions only myself as my mother's daughter, and one Betty Burke, Irish-seamstress-about-to-become, and is written here clear, to be accompanied by Neil MacEachain alone.'

O'Neil and the Prince both looked at the handwritten missive as if it were demanding a personal debt from them.

The Prince spoke, a whisper, in a way that suggested the subject was not present. 'But, Miss MacDonald, to leave Captain O'Neil now, in this winding retreat, would be a loss to my safety, I am sure. God knows how much I appreciate every one of you, and I take not my fortune lightly on my heart to have each of you by me, yet it seems wicked reward to abandon this soldier here, especially with forces landed who would be so mischievous to him if his history came known.'

'I understand, sire, but see the letter, which is set and unchangeable, this passport is your escape; if we are to be threatened with challenge and with arrest – as most likely we shall be – this letter fits perfectly our shape as a party. It is to Captain O'Neil they would raise enquiry, as to who he is and why he accompanies us, and place greater attention to each of our identities.' The delivered hammer blow then came from her: 'Also, he doesn't have our language at all.'

O'Neil turned to her, seemingly using a more private voice. 'I see your sense, and I would never risk the endeavour, though my instincts are to protect you all.'

The Prince gave MacEachain the eye, for they determined that O'Neil served both his flame for this well-shaped lass as well as his loyalty to the Prince, who tried a weak diplomacy. 'But our oarsmen are not so named on the letter, Miss, and they shall be with us.'

'Yes, sire, but the letter will truly operate after the landing, when we must let the boat away with the men, giving you no retreat by water, but the better to leave no trail of your arrival on the island. Heaven help we are not to be intercepted at sea – that would be ghastly enough – yet we are more than likely to meet some guard, devout to monitoring and observance on the roads of Skye. Mr MacEachain and I both were put to arrest just a short time ago, and only intervention of my stepfather put us at our liberties.'

O'Neil said, 'I am indifferent to all aspects of my fate, so long as Your Royal Highness's fate is to be at liberty. I will leave. As you formulate well, Miss MacDonald, we are under protection of the letter alone, and even at this moment I am become an encumbrance to you.'

Miss MacDonald seemed alarmed by that choice of word, but perhaps the hopeless fellow spoke the straight truth in more ways than one.

'Never an encumbrance, my dear O'Neil,' the Prince corrected, 'never that. We shall join again in the year that comes, we two shall ride side by side at front, with an army behind us, as we did in those months past.' He took the Irish captain in an embrace, so the decision was made. 'Seek John O'Sullivan among these wilds; as you witnessed,

I said these very same words to he, us both weeping.'

'Yes, sire, your journey will be onward until your just liberty is assured with a French voyage.'

The Prince reminded him, 'Unlike I, your French officer commission shall keep your life, sir, if you are seized, but take care to yourself.'

O'Neil gathered his ball of canvas, secured at the top with a tie, and they accompanied him outside where the MacDonald brothers, with MacMerry and Campbell, stood smoking. They gave O'Neil best guidance on the most occult walking routes back south from that shoreside. The Prince embraced the man one more time in this world, and he covetously parted with some specie or coin from his purse, to aid his poor future. The last thing O'Neil did was nod curtly before Miss MacDonald.

❧❧❧

Rid of O'Neil, the others kept outwith the bothy, leaving Miss Flora and the Prince alone while she unfolded the items bound in the rug.

'Well, Miss, I am ready to become as new, but first secure me as I am, so I can return to my former self with these clothes, which came also from your Lady Clanranald. We must hoard them safe.' The Prince began to strip away his clothes before Miss MacDonald. 'You have become my new tailors, as well as my guardians.'

'We have been at needle and thread for some days and had only your general dimensions, so I hope the guesses fit the truth.'

'Can you vouch for fashion, Miss Flora?' asked the Prince, raising his eyebrows as he peeled away his shirt.

'No. But strong stitching, yes.'

The Prince laughed, removing his shoes and stockings, his trousers and tartan long jacket, his waistcoat too, so he stood only in his breeches, articles which were the victims of brutal usage, though slightly redeemed by frequent, natural immersions in rain dousings, shallow stream baths and forded crossings, which he was ever pray to in these lands of his elusive flight.

'I fear, Miss Flora, you write a great role for me on the lit stage, but stands before you a poor actor.'

'No, no, sire.' She smiled. 'There is no stage. We must only form an impression devoted to the viewer from a distance – it is the *impression* of a femininity alone we seek, not true imitation.'

'True imitation would be a task beyond me, Miss Flora, though it is known upon the theatres and indeed in certain worlds beyond that there are men who pass veraciously as absolute women.'

'Indeed?'

'I have met such a one rumoured to be just this, and as fair as fair, a young . . . This in Paris, and I was . . . Ah. Well. Let us both to this task at hand.'

He stood naked in his underthings.

'Sire. Miss Betty Burke is an Irish spinner servant, and she is no more. She need not speak. Redcoats should not cast more than an eye glance onto your new form, for all they seek is, of course, a man. Your known form: a man, majestic and spruce.'

'Miss.' He smiled. 'You have adulated a fraction too much there. My physical person is in good health, but a little flustered and jolted about, I think – not having slept in real bed or proper bathed for many weeks, as you can witness. Look how the terror mitches have savaged at my legs.'

'A drooly plain servant girl serves the redcoats no purpose, sire. The eyes of soldiers scatter over their targets quick, seeking goal, and we want their eyes to pass on from you of a moment. We wish you to appear an irrelevance.'

'Well . . . so . . . an irrelevance I shall gladly be. And what is this?'

'It is a petticoat, sire, made by my own hand.'

'Yes, the same article, perhaps I have encountered one. Or two. I mean, glimpsed, in Paris. Or perhaps not, such matters overtake me in my accelerated life. I am mistaken. Not in passing. I mean, yes, in a glimpse . . . once.'

'Petticoats are petticoats, sire.' Stood before him, she was holding out the item with both hands.

'How is it attached? As a kilt?'

'No, sire. You step into it. It is an undercoat.'

'What faces, and what retreats?'

'It matters not; it is uniform all round. Shall I show you mine, how they lie?' And she made to display her tails in beneath her own dark tartan dress.

'Ah no, no, certainly not, Miss Flora. I apprehend.'

Turning then, Flora suddenly added, 'Ah, and this comes with us also.' She handed to him a small item wrapped in cloth. 'Disused by my stepfather, and the smith gave it a turn on his stone.'

Not to place it down on the earthen ground of the bothy, the Prince shouldered up the petticoat against his cheek and used both his hands in opening the small cloth parcel, to remove a wooden-handled, straight razor blade. 'A razor, to barber myself. I have one I use on occasion.'

'Yes, sire.' She smiled at him.

'Ah. But where?

'Where? Why, sire, where else but on Your Royal Highness's face, by custom? To shed your substantial beard.'

'Rightly so, yes. I shall see to it.'

'To clean your cheeks. For further reassurance of your impression of womanhood, though, we have a bonnet and veil here also, to fully shield yourself.'

'Certainly. Yes.' He put down the straight razor and, resigned, now stepped into the petticoat, pulling its waistband up his person.

'Good for length, sire.' She nodded with satisfaction.

'I trust all your judgements in these accuracies.'

'Now to the gown, formed from a calico we had fortune enough to have supply of. An attractive pattern of blue pliant sprigs, I hope you feel?'

'I am sure Betty Burke would think it a pretty thing.'

This made Flora chuckle, obscurely. She stood at his rear, to manoeuvre the gown into true position then secure it, before she came to his covered breast. 'Now to the mantle, which we affix encircling.' In these mechanics, the young woman's face came up close to the Prince's own, with her freckled fresh skin, her cap off – hair simply held back – fresh bistre eyes, focused on perfection of the garments' positioning. Her hands moved around him busily, adjusting matters.

The Prince monitored the concentration, the occasional blinks of Flora's eyelids. 'Miss MacDonald, are you a follower of the moon?'

Not meeting his gaze, small breaths emanating from her, as she rose and fell about his person, she spoke in a puzzled tone. 'I beg you give me pardon, sire, but what is your meaning? The moon?'

'Yes.'

'To the extent that it is not to be high tonight, for the needs of the crossing?'

'Ah, the danger for that sky-set illumination to reveal our ferry too clearly to observations and alarms?'

'Yes, sire. Is this your meaning? I talked of the moon

and weathers with Clanranald. We are prepared and aware of its influences at night, as are our sailor men.'

'I am convicted that you are. Its astrology is such in these high latitudes that it can make reading a romance book at midnight a daylight task.'

'It can be so.'

'Miss MacDonald. A delicate question. I can only compare, and I am quite ashamed how much I am depleted here, in the area of natural bosom, while aiming at convincing womanly qualities . . .'

'Sire. As we agreed one moment ago, the eyes of men must pass only swiftly across you, so modesty of charm in all given attributes is what we wish to maintain. Men can be singular and attentive in their direct appreciations. The less you possess to draw their eyes is all power to our cause.'

'Quite, of course. You have the wisdom there, Miss Flora. We move on.'

'Stockings, sire. Two stockings to draw on and up.'

He took the two stockings, and Miss MacDonald had to elevate the petticoats and calico at the frontage, grabbing a firm bunch to haul them high as the Prince leaned ahead, lifting his leg and drawing the first stocking up over his toes, ankles and calves. He grunted.

'Hoist them higher, please.'

The Prince complied.

'And to the other, straight, sire. Keep them straight.'

'Now, Miss MacDonald. It's of my devising that as well as my money pouch, which I can affix here, I can secure two pistols beneath these agglomerations here.'

'Your pistols, sire?'

'If they are well bound, I calculate that when seated, they could be very easily drawn; when standing, my removal of them might be hindered somewhat, but I am sure you or I can strap both . . .'

'A little higher now, if you would please, sire, if you will. The stocking must be up a little higher there to you.' The woman kneeled fully now, the ruffle of her own dress pushed down on his one resting foot, to monitor the operation. 'Not for any artfulness, as of course the stockings are hidden, but your want is to have them surely pasted onto yourself, or learn it is a woman's common derangement to endure them ever cascading down throughout a day, and I wish this on no woman. Or man. Pistol, you say?'

'In my present circumstances, you will understand I keep my two pistols close, at all times, and that must be so now. I will never be taken without resistance.'

She rose but kept the man's skirts hitched high in both her hands as she frowned at his spindle legs. 'It's a poor thinking to have them in this choice of placement.'

'But there they are to hand.' The Prince nodded to the pile of his belongings, and the very two pistols lay atop his kale bag in their holsterings.

'To affix them here is unsound consideration on several counts, sire. There is the matter of your true gait, for surely fixed there, like two hanging new lambs at suckling, they will influence your gait.'

'My gait?'

'Your feminine walk, sire. You must comport yourself in the ways of movement obvious to women, and there is the other matter, which, were you to be searched close by patrol, your primed weapons fixed here would discover yourself up to any searcher immediately.'

The Prince laughed and held back his shoulders. 'Miss MacDonald, if the fingers of mine enemy roam in such regions, there will be other discoveries for them than my two mounted silver pistols – there is risk they come upon a third pistol; unless we have the blessing of a very gullible searcher, the whole edifice of my disguise may be long realised well before the first hoist-up of my pretty skirts. I may as well accompany mine enemy on a happy bathing trip, *au naturel*, and expect myself undiscovered.'

The young woman smiled then she too laughed at this staunch sauciness before firmly beating down the petticoats and gown. 'Well, as a military lord, perhaps the razor blade hidden in there would be a substitute weapon?'

'That could carry its own unique hazards of movement fixed in this same place. How of this cudgel? A firm wood striker? I will take that to hand, small but weighty and excellent in use. I will affix that there instead.'

'As you think. These buckled shoes are to be Betty's to put on, please. Now to your finishing, this headdress and cap is affixed.' She placed the headdress and then enclosed it within the bonnet and lace, which when pulled forward, served to come in tight, burying the Prince's head and face deep within its lace edging. 'And we have incorporated a light veil, not so obscuring as to make it appear as masking, but, pulled across, it shall conceal you more.'

'And better, Miss Flora, it could seal against the torment of the terror mitches. Why, I begin to wish I had travelled in this form on the hills long ago, to resist the dual plagues, of both mitch and redcoat. It is a good warm uniform also. I feel it already.'

She smiled.

'But this headdress' – he blew from his mouth, to displace the smaller strands from around his lips – 'it is an ill fit, made for a smaller head than my own.'

'Try to maintain it straight.'

He attempted to fiddle with the hair, but the pelt fell forever forward upon his nose, and the mop fairly obscured him, so Flora laughed.

'Oh, Miss Flora. It is as to having a dead cat rest upon my scalp, instead of the crown.'

She laughed again. 'I think it is time to present you.'

'No, no. I fear my debut to the gathered men. Could you ask Mr MacEachain to enter first, to judge my rebirth.'

So, she called in MacEachain, who stooped to pass the

low doorway. The Prince stood still before them both, dressed as a woman.

MacEachain was silent, standing in judgement a few moments. 'But, Flora, where is His Royal Highness? He was here a short while ago, and who is this maid, suddenly come before us? Madam, to your acquaintance know I am Neil MacEachain, a schoolmaster of these islands. I don't believe we have met before?'

The Prince fiddled with his hairpiece. 'Very well, Neil, have your jest. God, this pelt. I thought me free of the terror mitches, but it replaces them.'

MacEachain laughed. 'A worthy transformation, sire, it is a miracle of theatre. Flora has done magic on you; you shall never be anticipated.'

'I am afraid I must show myself to the rowing fellows. I am as feart as a boy first lowered on a big horse.'

'Yes, let us test it upon their certitude.'

The Prince came with his escorts out from the low bothy, but in the moment of his first step, the feminine illusion was diminished, as he moved with firm, gawky strides and muscular, clumsy turns through the doorway, perhaps in an effort to assert his real nature and combat the illusion.

The MacDonald brothers stood with MacMerry and Campbell in silence as the Prince, in the transfiguration of Betty Burke, approached.

MacEachain announced, 'Gentlemen, this is Betty Burke,

an Irish servant and skilled spinner to Miss MacDonald.
I hope you show the civility we accustom to all.'

The four men looked unsteady in an attempt of
solidarity, to not reveal any outward mirth – but something
of their look and their shuffling displayed this struggle.

Campbell dared speak first. 'I have a loose button here,
Miss, if you are able.'

The other men trembled at the daring.

Roderick spoke up. 'Well, sire, there can be nae question you have passed to the other side.'

MacMerry let out a harsh sound.

The Prince quietly said, 'As a timid Irish servant to Miss
Flora, I shall keep my silence.'

'Sire, it is hard upon me: one thought, one strong
thought.'

'Speak it out, MacDonald.'

'What thinks you Captain O'Sullivan would make as a
speech to you at this moment, sire?'

Both the MacDonalds and MacEachain, knowing the
captain, laughed.

The masculinity of the voice emanating from within the
hood only added to the topsy-turvy of the predicament.
'A lady present, fellows, a lady is present, and O'Sullivan's
meditations would be contrary to her decency.'

MacMerry spoke. 'Two ladies present, surely two, or
are my eyes cross-purposed with the dram, yet I took none
the day?'

'Ha, what *would* Captain O'Sullivan say?'

'Were Captain O'Sullivan here, sire, your honour and rights of privacy might be in danger, for he often spoke for want of perfumed company. And you are from his own country now, ha, ha.'

There was more laughter.

'A lady present, sirs. I remind you. But have your mirth.'

The men chuckled openly, dissimulating that it was on O'Sullivan's account they laughed, but they looked at one another as young boys again, set on a dare.

'God's truth though, Miss MacDonald, and the thought never crossed me, a private word, if you please?'

'What is it, sire?'

But all heard his words as he fiddled on with his headdress. 'What when I am taken by the calls of nature, madam? On the field of campaign there are no places amongst we men for dedicated privacies; we have to let nature's course take precedence before one another, whenever needed – as is military custom – but what now? I fear I must fast of drinking already. And when the need comes, I will require a stunning privacy afforded me for the complication of the act which is suddenly new to me.'

All heads now turned to Miss MacDonald.

'Sire, I can say the skirt will not have affected any profound change in the mechanics of what is beneath.'

The men laughed. Roderick called out, 'Truth well said, Miss Flora. I mind her as a little lass, aye with wit enough.'

'But God's sake, all of you, I am sure to turn myself head-over-heel in the strange requirements of this dress. Hah, I will need a team about me, as for the dressing of a parade horse with saddle. So, laugh on, my boys, but that can be your duty to me: lift these skirts and stand clear of the guns.'

Through the long wait for dusk, to warm themselves, a fire from drift woods and lootings of bothy debris was lit back from the shoreline, angled between two higher rocks which acted to shield and delimit tightly the sweep of coordinates from which any flames could be observed.

Roderick MacDonald took on a watch from the elevations above them, and just as well, because within an hour he came hissing down from there. Four full wherry boats were a half-mile distant, loaded with armed men, coming up the loch. MacMerry used the splashing crockery dish filled with sea water to dash and douse the fire dead, then he kicked the cinders apart before he repeated another soaking to kill any rising steam. All the party ducked low and retreated far back into the heather, the Prince's skirts flying. Their mission seemed undone because of their boat, which was still pulled up in the small coving below, but within a half-hour, the full patrol returned and passed, without landing anywhere. And, in truth, many boats littered those shores at intervals.

They came back down to await final nightfall, but they did not dare relight the fire.

Chapter 8

U nder darkness to the south was the Sea of the
Hebrides, and before them was the Little Minch. East
was to the Isle of Skye. The man dressed as a woman was
ferried onward, striking out for another land across moonless
night water. The Prince often just stared ahead, like a gleeful
cartographer probing some uncharted archipelago.

In the still airs, the oarsmen were forced to row away
from the Uists for hours, but well after midnight a wind
and light rain came, so the sail was raised and this carried
them well enough on, until a hearty debate erupted in
Gaelic as to what precise direction they should be headed.
With no compass taken, the humour among the men grew a
little ill after this squabble. The Prince urged them forward.
He had removed his headdress and cap with the liberty of
being out at sea, so those items did not torture him.

He attempted to raise the spirits on board, and to entertain Flora, by singing. The presentation was assisted that his rather sweet male voice came out from a near invisibility, so his pantomime selection of dress was unseen. He seemed to particularly sing the words to Flora, who sat so close to him.

Whereby I can tell
That all will be well,
When the king shall enjoy his own again.
Yes, this I can tell:
That all will be well,
When the king shall enjoy his own again.

There's neither swallow,
Dove or dade
Can soar more high, or
Deeper wade,
Nor show a reason from
The stars
What causeth peace or
Civil wars.
The Man in the Moon
May wear out his shine,
By running after Charles,
His wain.

> *But all's to no end,*
> *For the times will not mend,*
> *Till the king shall enjoy his own again.*
> *Yes, this I can tell:*
> *That all will be well,*
> *When the king shall enjoy his own again.*

Later, Miss MacDonald, worn by the long journeys and the dangers of the preceding day, submitted to fatigue and slept, lying out in the bottom of the boat. The Prince took care to sit by her, ensuring the sailor men did not step on any part of her body as she slumbered, when they stood to adjust the sails. These trimmings had to be regular, as the wind was shifting round awkwardly; and when light began to show the isle off their starboard, more violent collisions and oppositions seemed to occur in the upper air, the wind and spits of rain having turned to work against them, so the men had to row into full resistance.

In full daylight, upon the waves, they came within sight of Vaternish Point; the wind dropped, but they rowed starkly adjacent to some shoreside sentries who they had not noticed until it was all too late for it. Those still figures, one in a grey coat but one in red, observed them from the shore, waved insistently to them, then went down towards their own boat; however, the tide was so low at that time there were clumps of seaweed and humps of wrack amongst the wayward pools, and it was obvious

their boat could not be launched without being physically
dragged several hundred feet outward from the shore. The
Prince's boat rowed on, and they were unpursued until, in
the calmer waters inland of the point, the men were given
ease at last.

The four rowers were so spent that there was no
choice but to come into the lee of high sea cliffs and rest
there a short while; the men leaned forward to recover
their breath among the rising and falling swell. Rushes of
quick water poured and broke from the wide flat tables
of stone on the rippling black surfaces at the bottom of
these huge cliff faces. Here, as they slowly gyrated, they
quietly ate some bread and butter in the dungeon-like
shelter, no one talking as any voice seemed unnaturally
amplified. In that parish of water, wide rolls of ripe kelp
undulated around them; beneath were vast undersea
nurseries of algae.

The magnitude of these cliffs, now so close and huge
above them, was a nauseating thing, putting far away the
comforting notions that among houses, formed fields,
tracks and hedgeways, as we walk to church, we move in
a world God fitted for us with snug accommodation,
adapted to the size and shape of humankind and rightly
appointed. But these were mammoth, uneven walls, up-
lifting, or in vertiginous lean, where miniature sky gardens
of pink sea thrift flourished in the horizontal seams of
stone, and nesting ledges smeared down hieroglyphics

of bird lime, as if this looming barrier was once erected in attempt to dam off the ocean itself, some colossal intervention of God, who had suddenly grown disinterested and abandoned the task, all the time thinking nothing of men in his makings.

Chapter 9

Bareheaded, maniac-hair sprung skyward towards the beech tree branches above him; cheeks flushed and discoloured, the man's face was scrawled in fury, lips snarling among an ill-formed razor shave which had clearly been self-administered while in a profound darkness. More monumentally alarming was the costume of woman's attire: dress and petticoat hoisted extremely high, perhaps bound there by string, revealing corkscrewed stockings, muddy lady shoes; and as he advanced on Mr Kingsburgh, a wooden cudgel was held threateningly in his right hand. 'Name your business,' the apparition demanded. 'You shall not leave if you mean ill.'

Kingsburgh was speechless. In the face of his regal imaginings, he now met a figure who looked like a refugee from a stricken theatre troupe, the acts of their already-wayward play blundered into some terrible catastrophe halfway through.

'Your Royal Highness. I am your Alexander of Kingsburgh, factor to Lady Margaret of Monkstadt, and her husband Sir MacDonald. I come down the hill with greeting from Donald Roy of Baleshere, who you know and is up by the house.'

'Ah, yes, MacEachain expected me of you. Donald Roy of Baleshere is here? He was with me at our army. I was by his brother Hamish of Baleshere just some time ago.' The figure had dropped his raised arm and seemed to immediately change demeanour into that of a common fellow, enthusiastic for gossip. 'Is Donald Roy well, sir?'

'Yes, Your Royal Highness. Though an injury to the foot from that last fight to defend Inverness heals poorly. Your Royal Highness, I bring bread and wine.'

'Ah, well, I am grateful for both. Shall we take some and jockey on somewhere?' To further corrupt the debased femininity, the Prince produced an unlit pipe, which was placed in his mouth, where he chewed and munched at the end for want of tobacco.

'Government troops are everywhere, Your Royal Highness. Officers are sat at Lady Margaret's Sunday table this moment, with the troopers stood out past the garden by the road there, jesting. But they have no comprehension you are here on Skye, such is the skill of concealment Miss

MacDonald operates. There has been parliament with your Mr MacEachain and with Donald Roy about the most secure means of forward movement for you, and we feel that to my home for now is best.'

'I am ever obliged and grateful, Mr Kingsburgh.'

'It is to my honour.'

'You will deduce from my disguise I travel incognito?'

'Incognito. I can see for the boat crossing you undertook that this adaptation of a woman's appearance would have been good business, Your Royal Highness.'

'I fear I make a desperate woman of gentility but being taken for an Irish hooley suits my abilities well. The role seems to work but has been untested beyond my protectors. How do I look to you, Mr Kingsburgh? As long as I am not encountered face-to-face, I conclude I pass at a distance relatively well as an Irish servant. It is the *impression* which counts. Don't have doubt I possess a headpiece adapted to cover my hair and face, which gives me as good as the itch.'

'Sir, I am sure I am unworthy as a critic of theatre.'

'Well, Mr Kingsburgh. We struggle hard enough to understand female kind. Surely, they are guided by the moon, so imagine the difficulties on me to become one?'

꩜

Early that evening, the Prince in costume strolled the open roads with MacEachain and Kingsburgh both, along the track round Uig Bay towards Kingsburgh House on the Loch Snizort Beag, where awaited him his first real bed of mattress and linen in months. They were overtaken on horse by Miss Flora, and Mrs MacDonald of Kirkibost, who had Kirkibost's maid accompanying on a pony. The riding party were headed onwards, making a cover and reconnoitre of what might lay over the roads ahead. Miss Flora still held the passport letter close, in case of intervention.

The maid of Kirkibost knew nothing of the operations afoot around her. Recognising what she thought of as one of her own dominion, Mrs MacDonald's maid gave a stern eye to the shocking, overgrown servant woman walking along by them, accompanying Factor Kingsburgh. Kingsburgh was a propertied man of canny high standing, and with him also for his walking companion was a sober-seeming Mr MacEachain. But the maid was affronted by the display of that . . . Irish servant thing, it was said to be, clearly with expectations far beyond her scrawny gifts. Even on a Sunday, the sniffen thing carried its skirts shamefully high in both hands. Crossing the low ford at Romesdal stream, it wholly leapt, like a hopping ewe, slapping its knapdallicks – with her starved dancer legs all a-showing in glaured and messed stockings, petticoat swishing, like a pintle-seeking-tumble-me-now-poxtrembler in a godless port city, rank with sin. Then, mighty Lord, the same skinnymalink, how it moved! God save us, it walked like an adrift coo with a deid stillborn hanging out the hole in its arse; this Irish grappler, loupen in malkin strides, it threw its lanking arms about as it strode – was it flies and clegs pestered at it? Doubtless drawn by its clart, aye, and here it was, turnin and gawping at every sight they don't have in all of low Ireland all about it, then ramming its heid low if you tried to get a glear in at it, so's ye would recognise it again about the island, or in Portree, and could mark it as a sure pongster.

Worst of all, it seemed to believe it had the liberty to walk alongside Kingsburgh himself, he who normally was a strident, upward fellow of gey guid sense – yet here he was, accepting of this strachled creature at his right arm, cavorting at his side as if she were his equal in this life, laying off there with elbows flung this way and that, as though debating matters of state and higher things than a bog trachle husbandless land-glaik could. The Prince of the House of Stuart himself was loose in these lands, with hardy troopers everywhere a-searching him and thirty thousand pound on his bonny head. Yet look at that thing, free-as-can-be, while nobility is hunted; why, thirty thousand to be had, but that mess would sell itself to a trooper out in the midden, and lift its skirt full, not for fourpence ha'penny. Damned foreigners. Silly daft hoor.

Kirkibost's maid passed on after her lady.

After some time, to the dismay of MacEachain and Kingsburgh, scattered parties of Sunday evening Holys, dressed in black, came the other way towards them, passing as they returned in from kirk towards the shielings round Uig. A people used enough to spotting a stranger on their isle, not one of them failed to mark, to monitor then stare upon this tall Irish spinning servant gallivanting at Kingsburgh's rear – having been ordered back there by MacEachain. The Prince strode as if he was still in the open moors of the flow country, unobserved. Each stride had his knees knocking the dress skirtings hither, wildly, like a fluttering bird trapped within a covering cloth, then, instead of diverting round each rain puddle on the track, the dress and petticoats shot up and he hopped the wetness onto a sturdy landing, maintaining the skirt's elevation if he observed another puddle still ahead.

MacEachain found himself emotionally trapped between helpless bouts of hilarity, where he had to hold his hand to his mouth at the entire predicament, but also gluts of fear and anger at the man's inability to accept stark advice. MacEachain hissed at him in temper, 'For God's sake, sire, take care what you are doing, for you will certainly discover yourself.'

When the churchgoers were passed, the Prince advanced on Kingsburgh – not to his side, but cheekily walking a few steps behind him. 'Mr Kingsburgh, do I fail poorly at imitation?'

Kingsburgh replied, 'Sire, it is custom of the government to address you as the "Young Pretender". It is an ill name in many ways, but also as you are surely the worst pretender I have ever seen.'

Yet they arrived at Kingsburgh House without interception. And that night, before his fresh bed, the Prince – still dressed as a thespian – was in about a good few bumpers of brandy when Alexander of Kingsburgh asked the Prince what would have become of him had Kingsburgh not by chance been up at Monkstadt that day. The Prince aired the explanation again. 'But, Kingsburgh, sir, it was providence itself that you were to be there this day to spirit me away. I have all faith in such providence that I shan't be discovered up, and so many have been my tight escapes it can only be explained by providential manoeuvres. How else, sir, how else?'

And again, was it perhaps not so? This escaper's progress was clear: he always evaded capture, but it was a supernatural providence aimed at the Prince alone, for wreckage was left around him in all places.

Less than a week later, Captain Fergusson of HMS *Furness* came to Kingsburgh House with no invitation, accompanied by a sergeant and fifteen troopers who waited outside. Kingsburgh said to his wife, 'The captain has come to examine you about some lodgers you had lately in this house, so perhaps you could be distinct in your answers,' but she was evasive.

Captain Fergusson asked directly where Miss Flora MacDonald and 'the person along with her in woman's clothes' had slept.

'I know in what room Miss MacDonald herself lay,' Kingsburgh said, 'but where the servants are laid up when in my house, I know nothing of that matter; I never enquire anything about it.'

Fergusson leaned towards Kingsburgh's wife. 'Tell me then, please, madam, whether not you laid the Young Pretender and Miss MacDonald in one bed together – perhaps in innocence that passion would be unspent, and her every virtue assured, as it was merely one lady lying abed with another, her servant. Would that have been the libertine arrangements of the summer nights here?'

The lady replied, 'Sir, whom you mean by the Young Pretender I shall not pretend to guess, but I can assure you it is not the fashion in the Isle of Skye to lay the mistress and the maid in the same bed together.'

'I will reassure many real ladies, should they choose to visit. If you can really pound at your memory, madam, then please show me the room Miss MacDonald slept in, and also the room of her maid – so-called – on that night.'

When Fergusson returned to the hall, he said to Kingsburgh, 'I find it remarkable such provision is made for servants at this house; why, the rooms were of equal comfort. In fact, the maid's room was somewhat superior to that which Miss MacDonald reposed in. How strange. What a lucky visit for servants the world over is your house here, sir. I will inform all servants I meet where they might spend such a commodious and boon evening, should they visit with their masters.'

Kingsburgh bowed.

The military party left, but cruelly, one hour after, returned and Alexander of Kingsburgh was arrested – almost one year later he was finally released from Edinburgh Castle, where Captain Felix O'Neil had also found himself incarcerated.

Chapter 10

His disguise abandoned, now landed on Raasay, the orbid moon at far past midnight was strident. The Prince seemed to walk in transfigured daylight – a highly powerful but eerily precise light that appeared to examine every article on the silent island earth around him; it was as if an observant intelligence had placed the whole world and its every detail under the quiet scrutiny of its watch. While standing erect, he could see black ants on a large round stone moving in this celestial brilliance.

The Prince and two companions were casting shadows behind themselves, traversing the land in the still night, and the rough track took them through routed and denuded dwellings under that planetary glow. In the short fields the cones of the haystacks had been torched and hauled down, and their charcoal candour seemed made more satanic black in the light's acute insistence.

The corpses of cows, occasional horses, lay right against the dwelling walls, as if they had sought initial mercy there and were only fallen into a hypnotic sleep, awaiting some more vivid colour than this lactic flood to wake them from their dream spell – but with many, the fabrics of their dried flesh were sunk between their ribs, and an especially whitened bone pushed from one horse thigh, the hoof seemingly levitated in air against gravity's law.

The walls mainly stood, but the roofs were burned or had fallen in, and the sour smell of wettened charcoal was sharp. Household goods and utensils had been thrown outward at the front of some doors, then rampaged. The Prince saw a wooden bucket, the hemp handle deliberately sliced through, and even its sturdy bottom had been precisely hammered with forensic perversity, to render the object forever useless in all ways.

They came upon a blackhouse, the clod roof of which had been driven inward by somehow dragging a two-wheeled dung cart loaded with stones up and completely over the cottage, so the home's innards were ruptured and squeezed outward from its doorway and squat windows; torn fabrics and ripped, blemished canvasing extruded, like gasping tongues. Some few items of clothing were scattered, marked with unthinkable stainings in the moonlight.

To ensure their eternal redundancy, the two cart shafts that pointed to the planet Jupiter, throbbing in agreement with universal laws above that sunken roof, had been methodically sawn halfway up, and the poles of both cuttings used to ram and lever over a gable wall that had been toppled into rubble.

The Prince walked on with his two silent escorts on this grim circuit of patrol. At the bottom of the sloping brae, there was the debacle of another sacked croft house, utterly mutilated, as if a herd of apes fevered by rare possession had tumbled berserk in one side and out the other.

Here again there was the deflated essence of a horse, fabric laid on a frame, previously so starved that its flanks had not been flailed for meat, and next to it, the Prince saw a single collie dog lay slain, about which the maggots had done huge work. Close by, forelegs outstretched as if still in the art of diving, lay two dead cats, lifeless eyes now like dried black raisins, their ribs showing where they had been each pierced and hoisted on bayonet. They seemed to have been placed in this neat display, either from the hand of a grief-stricken carer, torn free of the scene – or conceivably, they lay displayed there in an arrangement of their own murderers?

This sight drove the Prince to a surprising and unexpected inner outrage – he had seen men slain with his own eyes, and here farm animals and dwellings were exterminated to punish and crush the culture of these peoples, to destroy any chance of recovery; a dog may snarl in protection of a master, and thus receive an unfortunate musket ball. But cats! And not even cats: the smaller creature was a one-month kitten. How could troopers recalculate the configurations of this world to such a conception where the massacre of a kitten conforms with just and manly action of war? The Prince stared down on the dead cats under the moon, recognising that these deaths acted as proof of the perpetration of some delirium, where men have moved beyond the cruel stratagems of dominion and entered a derogatory state of shame and self-detestation, a fury at the fundaments of existence.

These perpetrators, after bayoneting a small kitten, failed in their compulsions; for real continuity, they should have returned to that large rock where the Prince saw the moonlit ants, and each crawling insect should have been similarly and meticulously executed, one by one, by musket discharge, to carry this demented philosophy to its just terminus.

Yet the Prince's thoughts failed to establish the chronology of waypoints of logic that would succeed in fully connecting the atrocity he saw around him to his own presence in this new country. For him, these barbarities suggested a pre-existing aberration in the establishments of his enemy; like all of us, he found it hard to suggest to himself that by stepping to the right or by stepping to the left, he had initiated or been culpable for anything which could have conceivably led to the two dead cats laid out before him, the summer grass they lay on made to look as if it was coated in winter spiderfrost in that moonlight.

Chapter 11

The air was very clear, the day mild, the waters of the long loch beneath astonishingly still. The mountainsides were reflected in those waters below, faithful and absolute, so every dimple and dapple of the braes became imitated and inverted on the dark water surface – it was as if the world was unsure which way up it actually stood, for the steady and gorgeous birdsong was unaffected by inversion, the sound had no top and no bottom.

Close to eight hundred feet above, on the Ben Alder screes, was a dipped grove of trees and saplings, shielded from the lower world, the stage set placed among an outcrop of tumbled boulders, some the size of travel trunks, some of horse carts, some of cottages. This eccentric den had seized boulders into itself, two levels: an upstairs and a downstairs, though there were no stairs –

only two ten-foot ladders formed from the nearby trees: one for ascent, and one for descent. The mountain slope was steep in its cant here, but the hidden chalet was made true along its propped ground floor by level-shaped log cuts, spread with pounded soil and woven mattings. Rope lengths as thick as on a mainmast sail were bound through an agreement of trees, to pull themselves together like a sheaf, and then above the second floor, a rough sack roofing was fixed, daubed with oily waterproof caulk.

A fusion of nature and of man, this refuge could easily hold six or seven bodies overnight, and ten visitors. At the back of the ground floor, formed from two vertical rocks at angles, a large oven of stone was presented, where a baking fire could burn all night, the smoke debouched upward in a natural channel of these boulders then gathered into a wooden flue. The fire smoke was unobservable by day, but there would only ever be a very rare government patrol in this domain anyway, so desolate and uninhabitable was it.

Ewen Cluny MacPherson, creator of this architecture, was on the top floor, sat with the Prince, laying off, as was his wont, for both men were in the dram. In the fair weather, the other lodgers there – Locheil, with his sore legs, Dr Cameron and others – had gone off down the land a little to sit.

Chief MacPherson poured another bumper for his Prince. Cluny's father was dead of a broken heart amongst their destroyed estate at Laggan, but there was rogue gold in the heather, and he poured another drink for this Italian aristocrat in his mad dwelling. 'Their law, as called, sire, is the law of straight streets and cities, and there are neither before my eyes in this place, nor in all my country here. It is their law as they want to use it; it cannae have existence here, sire, nor dominion on us. It is no a physical force here. They can come up this hidey-hole, and my far whispering posts will have them ten mile good away with my runner ahead, but they will no have us catched, because with our vantage we will be two mile away before they have halfway of our slopes. What are they to do? And what if they did come uphill at us here – ten of them, fifty, four hundred – do you think we will be feart to fight back in a land of no witness, where a grave is easy made? And then what? None shall escape, for my boys will chop them on their flight, so they send more – and what then? Even if they found this worthy skulk, and it is destroyed as we watch from the summits above here, we can come back in a month and make it again – do they dare leave a sentry in this lonely waste? They'll find them hanging chin down in a week.'

'I see your point on the law, Cluny, but some laws must be immutable, irrespective of place. This is revolution which we don't want, and there is law of God at least – the law of King George, of course, does not sit among my favourites, for that is the one which puts a price on my

head here, a price that was not put on the head of Lord
George or Lord Elcho, despite what they tell me of their
risks. Here is you, with all lost, sir, which I am sensitive to.'

'Your Highness understands what matters to me is my
Prince. The arrangement has aye been. We are an element
to ourselves with the enemy, Highness – oh, we so are. It's
a fierce puzzle for them, no for us; it is the very nature of
this mountain land itself, sire. The nature of it horrifies
them, which means they cannae ever command us here for
one hundred years. They cannae beat us in the long take,
sire. We can only beat ourselves – by losing who we are.
They would need to stop living every one of us by some
unspeakable means to geld us. Their law is no more to me
than an insistent bleat up here, an uncanny, desperate
thing. Our dominion shall no be defined, sire, by a judge
in London or Edinburgh toun. Law can nae mair tell us it
holds dominium than can a buzzard fly in here and tell me
no to take my dram.'

'I understand, Cluny,' said the Prince, who had heard
this thematic extemporisation before.

'We can see three mile south, leagues and more, and
if you take a walk up the top there, I think sure there
might be a wee view of London church spires.' He
chuckled.

'Yes, Cluny.'

They had been playing piquet cards on the upper floor
while the bread was baked by Cluny's two men below,

one of whom was formerly his horse breeder. The warmth was very pleasant, for that south-facing compound caught sun most of the day during that season.

'I enjoy to hear your thoughts on the future fighting, Cluny, and past. The fighting bothers me most of this affair, for we all agree I had to fight, and it has made the enemy hard on our people.'

'Could I have done Your Majesty better service if I had been present at Culloden parks? I have read Lord George Murray's word on it as ye showed, but a man can pick out one thousand imperfections on any battle, sire, including the ones of victory. People talk of the ground no being good for us there – that there were walls – but, sire, there were walls at the Glads Muir. Was it not ever the same ground as at Glads Muir and Falk Kirk and yon hall outside Penrith in England?'

'The same ground?'

'There was flat moorland bog and walls or obstruction there on every battle, and now they talk of the ground, like as we just tripped over and no more; but it was aye the bonny charge put paid for the government troops in this rising and before. Which is how we fought one another here in the olden times. Like as the land, sire, we are an other people that they couldna find control with. It was the swift charges of our Highland men that ever put them to flight, sire, no cannonades and ordered musketry, and they couldna fight the mass of us when we were mad and in

among them, like a swarm of bees round a woman at bath
– they dropped their guns and ran, being nothing with
sword, just a big show of musketry.' Cluny had placed his
cards flat on the box before and he reached out to just
touch them on their worn edges. 'And the great problem
is, they have beaten the charge once now, and the magic is
gone – it could be the charge for us is no more. The way
of war from now on may be neat, ceaseless skirmishes
from these hills. And politics action for you, sire, on the
bandits of St James's Palace. For more help will surely
come, sire. It may be from France, it may be from Spain,
but the song goes on.'

The Prince nodded. 'Murray wanted to make stand
over the River Nairn, or at least forward of the Culloden
parks upon a seam of land by a building called Card Ross.
Or Carden Ross. I will remember it from the map; I will
need to look again.'

'Aye, well, what's done. When the egg is broke, it is
broke all round it. If you had stood there and made
torments for their guns and cavalry to move over uneven
ground, it would have done no harm for your army in line,
Majesty, but it might no have changed things in the charge,
as that would be giving the same uneven ground onto your
chargers also. But Your Highness knows, I am aye of a
simple thing to mind in all battles.'

'And what is that again?'

'They are won and lost in two or three minutes only.

They can take days to align, go for a few hours of shufftying about, but the charge goes in, and the moments that follow are how the dice roll: shall these cards turn up good or ill for ye?' He tapped the wood box they had played on. 'No one can really assay their wishes on those few minutes which matter, sire; it's a hanging bird in the sky as how it goes.'

The Prince replied, 'This, commanders don't like to hear, so victory is accurately claimed and loss inexplicable.'

'It is all in a few minutes, and what controls those moments is out our hands, sire.'

'It is providence.'

'Maybe, maybe, I would not know what to call it, but the issue is how much we control what is in our command. Look at these other battles that myself and even you, Highness, have missed. I mean the banging on Loch nan Uamh. We are in September month here today, and in May month, after you were away from the battle of Inverness, was a big noisy action when the money came ashore. And so many gathered on the shore to spectate that the rascally Navy of King George put cannons onto the people upon the land and had them fair running homeward that day. I wish I had seen it all: the ships were banging all day.'

'It was such when I left France.'

'Aye, and we have the money.'

'Keep it good, Cluny, and if I am ever away from here, I shall be back with more, and we will be there in St

James's Palace with no battles at all. If we landed in the south and so unbalanced their nerve.'

'Ah, take good cheer, sire. Take good cheer and be glad. There will be nae boats there on Loch nan Uamh, sire. If you have to dig in here for some of the winter, it will be the way of it.'

'They say the Isle of Mull may be my next place of hope.'

'Word will come down my lines, sire; you shall be armoured with these facts.'

One of the men, Cluny's piper in fact, called in Gaelic from above them, seeming like the voice of God from on high. This was because the watch could descend the rock escarpment directly over them, to call down through the canvas and leaf roof, and speed the telegraph.

Cluny shrugged as the Prince looked up. 'Only the messenger comes uphill towards us, as usual, sire. A bit swift in the day, but he comes.'

Yet this messenger carried urgent news which was thrown all about. He called it aloud before he had even entered the dwelling, as he had met Lochiel and Cameron lower down the slopes. Cluny turned to the Prince. 'Sire, it is in the utterly contrary to what I just spoke a short moment ago. That is of remark. Two French vessels lie in the Loch nan Uamh.'

The Prince looked aghast. 'Two ships at rest there. But how so?'

'He is unsure, sire, but the command involves a relation of Mr Thomas Sheridan's.'

'Ah, this is Michael Sheridan, I am certain of it.'

'I think your carriage awaits, sire. We should be off directly – it is three or four days' walk, depending.'

Chapter 12

It was as if God or the Devil had made a pier of stone for his feet to walk onto Scotland and then off. Strange that he should arrive, and leave forever, on the stepped tongues of very flat stone at the top north shore of Loch nan Uamh. Fishermen casting their nets on the loch must have long known and used these perfect lozenges for berthing, even net drying, but that day, anchored out on the evening slick, was *L'Heureux*, a corsair of thirty guns and three hundred crew, and closer in, *Prince de Conti*. In that fair weather, there was something oddly tropical about the calm soft air, clear light and profusion of little inlets with a surfeit of still pool water resting against this open stone coast.

In a tender, the overall commander of both vessels, Colonel Richard Warren, was oared in and came ashore to meet the Prince's entourage, explaining that both vessels had only been able to remain at anchor there so long because savage weather off the west coast had kept the Navy from patrolling; however, the weather had lifted and they needed to be off. As a jolly boating party by the sea, it was decided there and then to form a return ferry.

Cluny was to stay. The Prince would not see him for a decade, much of it, for MacPherson, spent at his mountain eyrie until he was pulled over to France. Old Lochiel, Dr Cameron – who was to be executed on a mission back to Scotland – Lochgarry, (brother to the spy), the poet John Roy Stuart . . . all were loaded aboard the oar boat as the Prince stood on the flat rock. A few local people, who happened by this odd staging post, stood watching these events, and one of Cluny's runners was there by him. It was they and only they who saw what happened.

The Prince was kissing Cluny as an equal, and embracing him – after all, he was leaving him in charge of a great deal of money with which he wished to buy the kingdom as his own on return. From within the boat, Colonel Warren himself reached up to take the Prince's arm, and the Prince put his right foot on the wide gunwale and then lifted his left foot to step into the boat, but the very low swell dropped slowly, so in a spontaneous act, the Prince put his left foot back onto the rock. It seemed, for an instant, he might step again onto Scottish ground, perhaps to embrace Cluny once more, or even so moved that he could not depart, but the low swell itself now gently arose and thus the Prince's foot was elevated up off this part of the world, not by his own volition but by the motion of the world itself, and here the Prince used that subtle, almost unnoticeable propulsion to step down deeper into the boat.

The oarsmen to the shore, who had held the boat with their own hands against the rock, probed their blades onto the stone and applied pressure to drive the craft a little outward, swirling the still water, then the oarsmen to the starboard began to row and swing the bow round so it pointed towards *L'Heureux* at anchor, and, like that, he was gone. The party of men aboard now sat still, their heads drawn to the sight of their next concern.

Two poor local fishermen, nameless and unlettered as such men always are, stood back from the shore there, idly watching, as in many classical paintings of sublime sights wherein two ideal watchers might be seen, thinly figured, somewhere in the shadows – a small detail added, watching, reporting to no one on these occurrences, but eternity itself, forever held silent.

These two men knew little of the swell figures they had witnessed, who was who, and why they were there, and why they had turned their society into a slaughter chamber. They knew one of those men was said to be the Young

Pretender to the throne of nations. They had been told the knowledge by a passing pedlar, and it explained the grand foreign ships out at anchor, but the two men had been ignorant of which of those men they stared at might have been the Prince, and their speculations had leaned to Dr Cameron.

Sometimes over the coming years, in humble places of worship, these two watchers were to hear words spoken of a similar tale of a man, another fisher of souls, who came among a people with promissory of things to come and then left them again with a definite assurance of return and of glory. Yet neither the Prince nor the fisher were to come back among their peoples, whether their people waited forever or whether they did not wait, whether they cared or did not.

Afterword

On 16 August 1745, the first hostilities between
Jacobites and government troops occurred in the
Highbridge Skirmish. This small conflict took place
initially at the now-ruined bridge, built by General
Wade, that crosses the steep-sided River Spean, close to
the modern village of Spean Bridge. Two companies of
the 2nd Battalion of the Royal Scots were marching from
Fort Augustus towards Fort William on Wade's road
when they were ambushed by just eleven men of Clan
MacDonald of Keppoch who blocked the south side and
sent the Royal Scots – around eighty-five of them – into
an ignominious retreat.

Though a romantic sight, and despite being of huge
historical significance, the Highbridge today is uncrossable
due to its shameful neglect and the collapse of its upper

sections in 1913. To visit the site, one must choose between the north or south sides, with the steep ravine of the River Spean below.

In the winter of 2016, Paul MacDonald, who is an Edinburgh-based expert in historic weaponry, visited the Highbridge, accompanied by his young daughter. MacDonald decided to visit the south side, with the sensible hunch that perhaps more musketry was discharged from the government troops on the north side towards the ambushers on the south, rather than the other way round. He had a new metal detector with him that day, and it was his first time operating the device. He switched it on and began sweeping optimistically over the ground, close to where the bridge opens out on its south side. In just a few short minutes of this very first sweep, he received a positive indication. Reasonably expecting some piece of modern debris, he prised up some earth close to a mossy tree root and, to his astonishment, easily lifted in his fingers a perfectly preserved lead musket ball which had lain undiscovered in that spot for over two hundred and seventy-one years and was last touched by the government soldier of the Royal Scots who loaded and fired it lifetimes before.

Mr MacDonald's wonderful archaeological experience at Spean Bridge is a good example of how legendary historical events can suddenly manifest themselves as chillingly real. These episodes, which we visualise in our heads and call 'history', really happened to living, breathing humans. This is the challenge of 'historical fiction'. In a way, this short book is my first attempt at 'historical fiction'. Yet I wonder if all fiction writing is in fact historical fiction. Even if I set my novel last week, it is still a form of historical fiction. Also, perhaps all 'non-fictional' historical writing which attempts to illustrate a narrative is also fiction? By which I don't mean for one moment to demean good historical writing. All the best history books which I have loved have told a pulsating, compelling story. But narrative is the issue. To write history is to reveal a narrative unknown to the subjects at the time. Even science-fiction novels and stories are intensely aware of history being projected forward, or of 'alternative histories'.

Writing about 'Bonnie Prince Charlie' has been a powerful, even overwhelming experience for me. I know, intimately, some of the landscapes this fiction is set in. I know of the incredible, surreal events which happened among these landscapes, but the historical sources often produce as many alternatives for a fiction writer as they do certainties. My feelings about Charles Edward Stuart are revealed in my writing. A chancer who brought havoc?

Yes, but who are not chancers who bring havoc, including all of us today? Like most aristocrats building their hegemony, Charles was just a brigand, but a fascinating one. We live in times today where we all seem so very sure of our beliefs and our civic virtues; we have never been so certain we are not sinners. Yet what would we all do if we really believed we each had God's will behind our more dreary aspirations for our two new cars, dinner sets and tarred driveways, and our personal concepts of what we and our families are entitled to? And what if we, too, could raise followers in our cause?

In writing about such historical periods as 1746, surely the single common denominator, the fundamental mystery which burns under what we are all trying to answer as writers, is simple: what was it *really* like? And, of course, it was slightly different for everyone who was there – so how do we find any unifying subjectivity?

For a fiction writer trying to portray this mystery of the past, it is frustrating, especially when we try to deduce what it was like for real people, for the 'great men' and women of history, and also for the often silent, untitled poor people. Our writing becomes based on other writings, for what else do we have but imagination? Of course the 'Jacobite fictional tradition' goes back to Walter Scott and *Waverley*, through Stevenson, Cosmo Lang and D. K. Broster. But I can see they struggled with the same conundrums. The limited, often staged photographic record of the American Civil War still fails to convey the experience, and as we move further back into eras before film, before photography, before audio-recording, the fiction writer journeys deeper into mystery. What did the Prince really look like when he was twenty-four years old? How did his spoken voice sound? How did men and women really sound when they spoke to one another in 1746? Fiction writers must ask these questions, perhaps more intensely than historians. Letters rarely reveal how we actually speak in our daily conversations. What did it sound like when Charles Edward Stuart and the most able commander of his army, Lord George Murray, had a conversation in English? It happened, and I would give anything just to hear it on a tape recording. It's my duty to try and imagine it, but doing so is also impossible. Any intense consideration of the distant historical past, and of human action, always produces two uncomfortable, simultaneous conclusions: they were so like us, and they were so unlike us.

When we really meditate on these matters, we are meditating on the nature of human reality, of perception and memory – yet, at the same time, these are but pretentious matters in that world of action and violence which we also know was all too immediate and real.

Concocting this short chronicle would have been impossible for me without key texts which I have heavily leaned on and need to acknowledge, some of which I have

known and loved since I was a young teenager: John
Prebble's *Culloden* and *The Highland Clearances*. Other
sources were Fitzroy Maclean's 1988 biography, *Bonnie
Prince Charlie*, Eric Linklater's *The Prince in the Heather*
and Frank McLynn's *Charles Edward Stuart: A Tragedy in
Many Acts*. I looked into the Reverend Robert Forbes'
remarkable *The Lyon in Mourning*, edited by Henry
Patton, which Miriam Gamble told me about, and I thank
her. I was shamefully ignorant of it. Andrew Lang's *Pickle
the Spy; Or, the Incognito of Prince Charles* was read
many years ago, though I didn't have a copy around.
Winifred Dukes' *The Rash Adventurer* has always coloured
and shaped my perception of the period. John Lorne
Campbell's *Highland Songs of the Forty-Five* always has its
moments of beauty. Robert McGeachy's *Argyll, 1730–
1850* is always to hand. Robert and I were pupils of
Donald Clark, head of history at Oban High School in the
late 1970s, a wonderful teacher who fired an interest in
the period for both of us.

In Chapter 4, I have freely borrowed from Hugh
MacDiarmid's translation of *The Birlinn of Clanranald*,
by Alasdair MacMhaighstir Alasdair. My thanks for
encouraging words to Alan Riach, who has recently
published his own new and exciting translation of the same
remarkable poem. In the rainy night sequence of Chapter 6,
as Charles Edward Stuart crosses the bogs, I seem to have
been propelled by Samuel Beckett's *How It Is*.

I have to thank my good friend Kenny Lindsay for his Gaelic contributions to this text. I also have to sincerely thank Jamie Crawford and Alison Rae of Polygon for including me in the Darkland Tales series, and for their brilliant editing, as well as their huge patience with me as I tried to find time to write. I wish there were more bold ventures like this in Scottish publishing.

We both reveal and obscure as we proceed in these matters. What is the truth? I recall J. G. Ballard in London once suggesting to me, 'We fictionalise to reach a truth.' I believe he was right. By inventing, I hope to make the elusive, in fact the surreal, nature of 1746 appear truthful. Thus, this chronicle now seems 'true' – at least to me – in my constant and garish dreams of that incredible, often horrible time.

Alan Warner
Killundine
Sound of Mull
February 2023

In Darkland Tales, the best modern Scottish authors offer dramatic retellings of stories from the nation's history, myth and legend. These are landmark moments from the past, viewed through a modern lens and alive to modern sensibilities. Each Darkland Tale is sharp, provocative and darkly comic, mining that seam of sedition and psychological drama that has always featured in the best of Scottish literature.

Rizzio Denise Mina

Hex Jenni Fagan

Nothing Left to Fear from Hell Alan Warner

Columba's Bones David Greig autumn 2023

DARKLAND TALES